THE LIONMAN KIDNAPPING

EVE LANGLAIS

Chimera Secrets 3 - Romantic Horror

PROLOGUE

THE ANIMAL CREPT CLOSER, SLINKING LOW TO the ground below. The dappled fur helped it blend with its surroundings. A lone wolf strayed from its pack. Prominent ribs showed its hunger. A predator who had started creeping much too close, sneaking from the woods at night for the more civilized areas, seeking easy prey.

And it would find it. Stupid two-legged things walked around without a care in the world. If the wolf attacked one, the rest would panic.

Best to handle the situation before shit happened.

The perch in the tree didn't prove very comfortable. The branch was barely wide enough to hold an adult body and not snap under the weight. Still, it provided the element of surprise.

The wolf never once looked up. It kept creeping, body slunk low to the ground as it aimed for the bunny placed in a makeshift pen. The tiny bundle of life no longer waggled its pink nose. It froze into a furry statue with long ears.

A wolf didn't hunt by movement alone. Its nostrils flared, inhaling the scent then following it. How sweet it smelled.

Yummy, yummy in the tummy.

The allure proved all too easy to comprehend. The tempting fast flutter of a heart. The slow, measured hot huffs of breath. The wide eyes staring, the animal too scared to even blink.

Yet there was something even more tempting than a delicious-tasting bunny, and that was the adrenaline of dominating a wolf. There was danger in hunting it. Thrill in the possibility of injury. And the most exciting rush of all, fighting to live—and winning.

The wolf passed underneath the branch, and it took but a simple lean to the left to fall out of the tree and land on the beast. It yelped then growled as its stiff hackles were gripped in two fists. Hitting the ground hard, it took a moment to recover. The wolf squirmed and snapped, slavering teeth coming close to flesh.

Grabbing the muzzle and shutting it took a bit of

straining. Legs locked around the body kept it from twisting. It took a firm arm around its neck before the struggles eased.

The body went limp. Then perfectly still. Only then was the wolf released, to be slung over a shoulder and brought back as a prize.

It would make a great rug.

CHAPTER ONE

"HE'S BACK AGAIN," ADRIAN—MORE COMMONLY known as Dr. Chimera—announced pointing to the video paused on the screen. Daylight poured into his office, the wide windows on the top floor providing a spectacular view of the mountains. Or so he recalled. It had been a while since he'd taken the time to admire anything.

Dr. Aloysius Cerberus—known as the boss's hell-hound behind his back—frowned. "Are you sure it's him?"

"Quite." Adrian knew all of his patients. His projects. Part of his curse was to never forget.

And I shouldn't forget those that I used to get where I am today.

"But why?" Aloysius pondered aloud. "It makes

no sense. Marcus escaped. We lost him. Why put himself within reach?"

Damned if Adrian knew. Yet there was no denying the image on screen. That face. The long, tangled hair notwithstanding, there was no mistaking the green glow in those eyes. "The last time his tracker sent out a signal he was a hundred miles from here." And then they'd lost him.

The projects that escaped the Chimaeram Clinic kept finding ways to bypass the implanted chips. It made locating them when they fled the clinic's care a challenge. Good thing they kept coming back.

"Could he want us to catch him?" Aloysius mused aloud. The man was looking trim these days. His ebony skin smoother than before, the gray along his temples less pronounced. Someone was self-testing with success thus far.

But Adrian had to wonder how the doctor dealt with the side effects. Because there would be some. All of the remedies came with a price.

More like a curse. A thirst for things forbidden.

"Could be he's hungry and having a hard time scavenging for food," Adrian offered. "Winter is coming. Perhaps a part of him remembers being warm and fed while living here."

"Possible." Aloysius rubbed his chin. "That

would indicate he's retained some of his memories, which is interesting."

Very interesting because usually those who escaped turned feral, losing their humanity and giving in to baser instinct. Some days Adrian wanted to join them. Staying human was a constant battle, and the blackouts were becoming a problem.

"If he's got some sense of his past, then I doubt he wants to return as a patient." Adrian spun his chair to look out his window, staring at the forest as if he could see the escaped patient at its edge.

"Could be he is cognizant enough to realize he needs help."

"From us?" Adrian couldn't help but snort. "After what we did, I doubt he's coming back for more treatments." The people he helped didn't always appreciate it.

Maybe you should have asked permission first. He had in a few cases. But in the interest of secrecy, he'd not been entirely truthful with what they were agreeing to.

I misled them. No wonder they hated him. He hated himself.

"You can't be sure of that," Aloysius argued. "Marcus was broken when we found him." A man in a coma about to be sold by his mother for parts. They saved Marcus at the eleventh hour and fixed him, only to break him again.

"And now he's bitter," Adrian reminded, because Marcus, like many patients before him who'd arrived at the clinic broken and desperate, turned on those who gave them a second chance at life. Reviled the science that saved them.

Surely a few side effects were worth the price?

Is it? Adrian tucked his trembling hand by his side.

"You think he's after revenge?" Aloysius said, his lips a grim line.

"Can you think of a more plausible reason?" Everyone needed a reason to get up in the morning. "Given the danger he poses, I'll send out a memo to halt all outdoor walks by the staff."

"Forbid them and they'll start bitching," Aloysius retorted. "Better if you tell them we've got a wild animal situation."

"Been having a lot of those lately." Adrian recalled their faces, too. Especially those of the dead. A reminder of the failures piling up at his feet. Never mind the many successes; it was those he lost that haunted him most.

"Has he strayed from the woods yet?" Aloysius asked, snaring the mouse off his desk to play the video in slow motion, slide by slide.

"No, but if he does, the guards will shoot." They didn't have a choice. The guards weren't about to sacrifice themselves trying to capture an experiment gone wrong.

The projects that escaped had a tendency of going quite feral. Only a few managed to retain their sanity. Some days, Adrian wasn't sure he was one of them.

"Are you having them use tranqs or bullets?"

"Bullets. We can't afford to lose more staff." Already there were questions. Whispers among the staff as they noticed their numbers diminishing.

"Are we sure he's feral?" Moving from the paused video to the sideboard, Aloysius poured himself a drink, well acquainted with the decanters kept in Adrian's office.

"Yes, I'm sure. Did you see him?" Adrian had studied the videos of his returned project over and over. Unkept, crouched, his every movement animal-like. The problem with splicing a beast's genes with humans? Sometimes the beast took over.

What do you mean sometimes, boyo? his inner voice taunted.

Aloysius waved a hand. "Doesn't mean Marcus is irredeemable. I dare any man living off the land to not appear as if related to Bigfoot."

"You're talking as if you think we should catch him." Not everyone deserved redemption.

But Aloysius wanted the failed project back. "We should at least make an attempt."

"And if we fail? He's a menace to the staff."

"No worse than Luke was," Aloysius shot back. "And yet you kept him around."

"Luke is a special case." One of the first broken soldiers Adrian had taken under his splicing wing. The man who'd endured it all. The one who made Adrian believe that perhaps he might pull through. If only he could convince the voices in his head before they acted.

"Could be Marcus is special, too. Don't we at least owe it to him to try?"

They owed Marcus many things. "What are you proposing? Send a force to flush him out?"

Aloysius shook his head. "The forest is his hunting ground." Every time they sent a group of people in, not as many came back out. "We need to draw him out."

"How? By putting out a plated steak dinner?"

"Maybe. We just need the right bait."

"Bait? You mean dangle someone in front of him. What part of 'we're short on staff' did you not grasp the first time?" Adrian's tone turned slightly testy.

The joys of being in charge and yet feeling as if everything around him spun out of control.

"I wasn't talking about using the staff. The nurses we've got might be made of stern stuff, but they're not equipped to deal with Marcus."

"So who then? A guard? Because you know they're not going to try and talk to Marcus. Not after what happened when he escaped." The one way to unite people against others was to spill the blood of their comrades.

"You know who I want to call."

Adrian's lips compressed. "I don't think that's a good idea."

"Is this about the wolf pelt again?" Aloysius rolled his eyes.

"Stretching it in my shower to cure it was not cool." Not to mention he had a moment where he might have squeaked when he saw the eyes starting at him when he went to pee in the middle of the night.

"I promise no fur rugs this time. Just a capture."

While the doctor was intent on making this a nonlethal maneuver, Adrian had his doubts, which was why he had a squad ready to go, their tranquilizer guns replaced with bullets.

Because maybe sometimes it was kinder to put the monster out of its misery.

CHAPTER TWO

THE DISCOMFORT OF MANY LEAVES STREAMING rainfall onto him in a steady deluge was ignored in favor of stealth. He didn't shift one bit as he watched from the woods, biding his time, doing his best to not forget. Trying to remember why he spied.

The big stone structure held his gaze, the color of it pale and accenting the big straight-edged rectangles that glinted. *Those are windows.* A way to see inside the building, an unnatural cave that housed the prey.

All around the lair, meat sacks roamed. They guarded those inside the building, their appearance and manner familiar somehow. Their fluting call among each other almost understood.

I used to be one of them. One of what? He

couldn't say. Another thing forgotten. The holes in his mind kept widening.

I am... The name eluded him for a moment. Who he was, a thing of the past. An almost forgotten memory. The answer struggled to rise to the surface of his mind.

I am Marcus.

But at the same time, he wasn't. Marcus used to live among the meat sacks. Slept in a bed. Wore clothes.

Then something happened. Something that he remembered only as raw pain, the kind that brought a low, rumbling moan to his lips. Quickly followed by anger.

So. Much. Rage.

It quickened his breath. His nails dug into the ground, gripping him in place lest he go charging across the open field. He'd seen what happened to animals that dared cross that...expanse. The sharp crack was heard after the creatures hit the ground dead.

Marcus dropped into a low crouch as he heard a strange whirring noise. A sharp glance overhead showed the giant metal bird in the sky. Its blades spun, its belly full of meat sacks.

Across the field, on a massive smooth surface,

there were more of the prey awaiting the arrival of the giant bird. One of them wore a white coat.

A doctor with ebony skin and a friendly smile.

A liar.

The bird—*no, that's a helicopter*—landed in the distance. Every day, sometimes twice a day, it arrived, disgorging new passengers, carrying away others. Guarded by the meat sacks in black who carried guns.

Marcus remembered guns.

Bad things.

Stay away.

Far, far away.

If they're so dangerous, then why am I here? The thought quickly turned to, *I need to hide.* Hide before the men with guns spotted him.

About to leave the edge of the forest, he paused and inhaled deep as the wind carried so many lovely scents. That of the crisp air, haunted by the coming winter, the acrid burn of fuel, and then the even fainter scent of the meat sacks. One of them more intriguing than others.

It caught his attention, and he turned back to look and noticed the last passenger to exit the helicopter. He blinked at what he saw. Then smiled.

Smiled wide as he saw the doctor hugging a dark-skinned woman. And even when the embrace was done, he kept his arm around her.

Who is she?

Someone important.

Someone the man in the white coat loved.

Marcus didn't have anyone to love. He had nothing.

Because of that meat sack. *I want to kill.* However, the doctor was too well guarded for Marcus to get close and he never strayed anywhere near the woods.

No one came to walk under the shadowy boughs anymore. Not even a crunchy guard.

And Marcus would know. He'd been watching for a while, perched still as could be by the forest's edge. Hours every day, leaving only to sleep in his den at night, pulled back to this place he hated.

Needing something...

He stared as the doctor eschewed the noisy things that moved quickly to walk with the female. He still had his arm around her. Stopped and gestured often, his expression clear and full of joy. Hers more reserved. Even this far he could see it, the smoothness of her features, the fullness of her lips. The juiciness of the rest of her.

She would make a tasty treat, only she disappeared inside, and not long after, darkness fell. He returned to his lair, his mind whirling more than it had in ages. Thinking. Planning.

The dawn after the helicopter landed, Marcus returned to the edge of the forest to watch. People strayed from the building, lighting tiny white sticks that smoked, moving in groups around a worn dirt track.

None of them proved interesting. He waited. The day passed with him only leaving his post to attend his needs.

The sun began to wane, and he started losing focus. Why sit here? What did he wait for?

He was ready to leave and hunt for his evening meal when *she* emerged. Immediately, he took notice.

Her clothing clung like a second skin to her body. Her dark hair was bound back, leaving her features clear. The white string dangling from her ear went to a box clipped to her waist. Even from a distance, he could hear the discordant jangle.

She paused to talk to a guard, the man in black pointing to the sky then the building.

The bad, bad clinic. His memories had become sharper since he'd started watching. The focus kept him alert.

The meat sack didn't convince her to return inside. Why should she fear? The sun might be setting, but it still lit the sky. She had time before dark. Bu not long before the hunters came out to hunt the night.

Marcus stood still and watched, memorized every line of her body as she circled around the track, jogging slowly past him. Never once glancing at the woods.

The second time she passed, he swore he got a hint of her scent. A tease that brought saliva to his dry mouth.

The third time, her gaze finally flicked in his direction. It felt as if she stared right at him, yet she didn't slow her pace and swept on past.

The fourth time, with the guard yelling it was time to go inside as the sun dipped below the horizon, he knew he had to act. Marcus would never get a better chance.

With twilight making it harder to clearly discern, Marcus stood and staggered out of the woods, just far enough to be seen. He let out a sharp cry and then fell against a tree.

In plain sight.

She might not have heard him, but the woman saw him and came jogging across the strip of grass. Yanked the buds from her ears. Her eyes wide with concern. Her features younger than expected. The skin so very smooth.

Her neck, small, fragile, bitable.

Marcus didn't lunge as she reached him. It wasn't easy to stay still. He could hear the shouting, his ears even picking up the distinct vowels. "Ma'am, get away from it."

It.

Had Marcus changed so much he didn't merit a him?

Cerberus was to blame. The coward who never strayed from his fortified castle. But there was a way to hurt him.

This sweet-smelling female held the answer to his revenge.

She reached into the pocket of her sweater, her voice a soft murmur. "Just stay still and I'll help you."

There was no help for him, only vengeance, and yet, he couldn't help but whisper, "Sorry."

Marcus suddenly lunged, yanking her by the arm, ripping her hand free from her pocket even as he dipped. A shoving of his shoulder into her midsection flung her onto him. Straightening his legs, he kept her braced with his arms, pivoted for the forest, and ran.

A feral grin lit his lips as he heard the shouted, "Holy shit, he's kidnapping her!"

CHAPTER THREE

ADRIAN WAS WITH ALOYSIUS WHEN MARCUS took Jayda. Literally. Just popped her onto his shoulder and ran into the woods.

"What the hell is happening?" Adrian snapped. "I thought I said no to your plan to use her as bait."

"You did." Aloysius frowned. "But you know Jayda."

Yeah, he did, stubborn and foolish. "I can't believe he kidnapped her." Couldn't believe and yet couldn't help an element of excitement.

"But you'll notice he didn't kill her."

Callous even by Adrian's standards. "This is not a case of half full, Aloysius. Why aren't you more panicked? We need to send the guards after them." Adrian already had enough blood on his hands. He didn't need to add one more name to that list.

"Not yet."

"What do you mean not yet? Why the fuck would we wait?" Adrian didn't often curse, yet the situation warranted it.

"Because his actions are odd. And we don't want to act precipitously."

It took strength to not pinch the bridge of his nose in exasperation. "He's kidnapped your daughter."

Yes, daughter, because Aloysius knew of a bait that would work, especially since he was not willing to put himself on the line. Then again, Adrian wasn't ballsy enough to offer himself as a dangly carrot either.

"An unexpected turn of events." If it weren't for the lines of stress on Aloysius' face, Adrian would have thought he didn't care.

"I don't suppose she agreed to a tracker?" Adrian asked. If only everyone would agree to be chipped, it would be much easier to keep track of people.

"Jayda wear a tracker? Not likely." Aloysius snorted. "She's still convinced she's invincible."

"She's not," Adrian said flatly. "I'm sending in the guards."

"Like hell you are."

Adrian glared. "I am not standing by and doing

nothing. As her father, you should be screaming at me to get men into those woods."

"Why the hell would I send men armed with guns after them? I know about their itchy trigger fingers. She might get hit in the crossfire. If that happens, things won't end well for them." A grim statement by Aloysius.

"We shouldn't have told Jayda about Marcus. You knew she'd do this." Then again, so did he. Jayda wasn't one to back away from a challenge. One day it might get her killed, possibly even today, and he would be at fault.

Don't tell me this late in the game I'm getting a conscience.

That wouldn't do. A doctor doing cutting-edge medical science couldn't afford to follow the rules.

Or get caught.

"Have a little faith. I'm sure she'll be fine."

"She was kidnapped by a lionman. How the fuck is she supposed to be fine?"

"Because she has to be." More of a fervent wish than an actuality.

However, Adrian wasn't about to wager her life on Aloysius's conviction that everything would turn out all right.

"I'm sending in the guards." Because the longer

they waited, the less likely they would find Jayda alive. And for some reason, that mattered.

CHAPTER FOUR

Don't let them catch you.

It was the only thought running through his mind, an imperative that had Marcus leaping and running through the treacherous forest. His feet nimble on the uneven ground. His breathing a huffing moist heat through his nose.

Over his shoulder, the solid weight of the female kept him focused. The scent of her surrounded him. Vanilla and honey with a womanly musk.

A woman who said nothing, didn't even scream.

Probably fainted, which was for the best. She wouldn't like what came next.

The means of his revenge wouldn't be pleasant. There would be blood involved. The lobbing of body parts in the direction of the clinic to let Cerberus know what he'd done.

Let him hurt like Marcus hurt.

First, he had to reach his safe lair, the cave he'd found, tucked into the mountain and hard to reach by normal means.

In the distance, he could hear the loud noise of vehicles in pursuit. The only way the clumsy meat sacks had any hope of catching him. He was much faster than them. Wilier, too, than those with no sense of smell or direction.

But the meat sacks had guns.

Mustn't forget those dangerous guns.

Lucky for him they weren't close enough to fire, and Marcus left them behind as he ran. He moved far enough away that the only sound was the whisper of his feet hitting the ground, the occasional stir of a branch from the wind of his passing, and the slight puff of his breath.

Still the female said nothing. Just dangled at his back, her legs under one arm, his other hand still grasping hers, holding her in a secure loop around his body.

Getting to his cave would be tricky with no fingers free to grip. He had to leap and hope his footing didn't slip as he traversed rock to rock, the calloused bottoms of his feet barely feeling the bite of stone.

Reaching the thin lip, he finally had to flip her

off his shoulder. He held her in front of him, noting her limp head, closed eyes.

Still unconscious. But not dead. He could hear the pitter-patter of her heart. Smell the life coursing inside her.

It smelled...divine.

He wedged her into the crack, pushing her ahead of him through the snug gap until it opened into a sizeable cave. Only then did he drop her—gently for some reason—laying her down on the floor, cradling her head. A wasted effort, given what he planned.

Marcus turned from her and crouched by the crack he'd just used. The only problem with his cave? It had one way in, which meant one way out. Yet it was the safest place he could find to hide and where he would conduct his revenge.

Seconds ticked by as he listened, strained to hear any signs he'd been followed. The silence, broken only by the soft whisper of wind, let him know he'd escaped the enemy. For now.

Which meant time to move on to the revenge part of his plan. He turned to get started, only to find the woman sitting and staring at him, holding out a square device that shone a light bright enough to see by.

She saw him, and for a moment, Marcus was ashamed. Could only imagine how he appeared.

Hair long, unkempt, and dirty. His clothes but ragged remains, filthy beyond any repair. His skin barely any better.

In direct contrast, she shone with cleanliness and good health. Stared at him with wide eyes. Opened her mouth, probably to scream, cry, or plead.

"Hi."

He blinked.

"Do. You. Speak. English." Each word succinct.

A frown creased his brow. "Don't talk."

Her mouth curved into a smile. "Well, what do you know. You do talk."

He growled.

"Too late. I already know you can. What's your name? I'm Jayda."

He didn't want to know her name. "Don't care." He turned from her, unable to look at her and maintain the rage needed to tear her to pieces.

"You must be one of the patients who ran away."

How did she know? He turned a sharp look her way. Narrowed his gaze. Of course, she knew. Look at who she kept company with. "Free."

"Can't say as I blame you. Those rooms can feel like a cage."

Despite himself, he found himself agreeing. "Bad place."

"A place of healing, you mean."

"Bad," he insisted.

"To some, I guess it might seem that way. But the doctors had reasons for what they did."

"Bah!" He snorted. What those doctors did to him...it shouldn't have been allowed. Wasn't actually. Not by law. They'd volunteered his body to experimental science, injecting him with a monster, and each day it was a fight to not let the beast sharing his mind win.

"They're really worried about you at the clinic."

At that, he couldn't help a feral grin. "They should worry." Because he hadn't yet completely lost his mind. Look at what a little focus could do. He spoke in words, not grunts.

"Are you dangerous?"

"Yes." Which was why she should show more fear. He glowered, and yet she continued to watch him, her gaze steady, the hand holding the light not even trembling.

"My dad wants you back."

Dad? So not wife or lover, but closer than that. Cerberus's kin.

The revenge would taste all the sweeter.

He took my humanity. I'll take his heart.

"Not going back." Ever. He'd rather rip out his own throat than become an experimental puppet again.

"Because living in this cave is so much better." Spoken with sarcasm.

He saw it through her eyes then, the dirty space with the pile of leaves against a wall. The smell of piss because he'd marked it against other predators. The discarded bones from a meal.

"I am free." Free of tests and medicine and a warm bed, with plenty of food. A cave was better than a cage.

"Free to be an animal." Definite sneer on her face and a reminder that the man was losing in the battle for dominance of his body.

"I like it." A lie. Marcus hated his life now, especially since the only time he was happy was when he wasn't himself.

"You'll die out here. Winter is coming."

He knew. Could feel it in the bite of the wind. And what would he do when it came?

"Quiet." He growled at her.

"Or what? You'll kill me?"

"Yesss." He hissed, flexing his fingers, the nails jagged and sharp.

"I don't think you will. If you really wanted to take me out, why not do it on the edge of the woods? Instead, you risked capture and took me to your lair."

A strange choice for sure. Had he ripped open her throat by the tree line, he'd have had his revenge.

The cameras would have caught it. Cerberus would have seen.

But he'd smelled her, and next thing he knew, he was running away with her.

"I will kill you." The words spilled from his lips, each one getting easier and easier.

"Really? How? Going to strangle me with your hands? Gnaw on me with your teeth?"

All of the above actually. "Shut up."

"Why should I? Not used to the things you kill talking back? Too bad, so sad, lionman."

The word caught his attention. "Not a lion."

"Says a guy who's obviously not seen his long blond mane in a while. Not to mention those teeth. Maybe you will rip my throat out with them." She angled her head. "What are you waiting for?"

What indeed? "Quiet." Because each time she talked, more clarity returned to him, and more conscience, too. It asked him how he could even think of killing an innocent. What had this woman done to deserve such an end?

"I won't be quiet because I don't think you know what you want."

How true, and yet at the same time, he remembered the reason why he woke this morning. Why he woke every day. "I want revenge," he roared, the words echoing in the small cave.

"Do you really think killing me will satisfy you?" She stood, and despite his size, she wasn't intimidated. She met him stare for stare. "Revenge won't be found living in the woods like an animal, freaking out the staff of the clinic."

"Killing you will hurt *him*," he huffed.

"Killing me won't do a thing to make it better. The thing inside you won't be satisfied."

"The thing inside me would enjoy seeing Cerberus suffer." The truest thing he'd said in a long time.

"Making him suffer doesn't help you, though."

"I don't need help."

"I'd beg to differ. Take a look around you. Is this really what you want?" She swept her hand. "Do you intend to live out the rest of your life like some base creature in a cave?"

"Better than being used as a guinea pig," he shouted back.

"It doesn't have to be the way it was. There are alternatives."

He almost asked her what she meant, only he heard a noise. His head swiveled, and he eyed the crack. His nostrils flared as the monster inside sniffed for danger.

"Lionman, eyes on me." Jayda snapped her

fingers, and he turned with a snarl to see her standing framed by a light.

A light created by a phone.

The realization hit him. "You sent a signal!"

"Actually, a whole message, but they're not listening to my orders." She sounded annoyed.

Not as annoyed as him. This was his secret place.

Which was why he barked, "Hands." Since he had no rope, he yanked off his shirt and spun it to make it into a rough cord.

She didn't offer her wrists.

"Give me." He reached and batted the phone out of her hand. It hit the ground, still glowing.

"That wasn't nice."

"You tricking me wasn't nice," he retorted, winding the cloth around her hands tighter than probably necessary, given she didn't offer any resistance.

Why did she not fight?

Why hadn't he killed her yet?

"Stay," he hissed, stomping on the screen of the phone, hearing it crunch and finally putting an end to its illumination.

He eased out of the crevice for his cave, just another shadow that moved slowly, quietly. The guard who actually managed to stumble into his area never heard him coming. Marcus felt no qualm about pouncing on him and knocking him out. No remorse at all when he dumped the body in a ravine nearby where it would take searchers a while to find. By then, he'd be long gone.

Marcus didn't expect to find Jayda still in the cave when he returned. Yet he loped back as quickly as he dared, scanning about for her scent, because she'd have left one behind as she fled.

She could try and run. He would track her and make her pay for disobeying.

Only...she remained in the cave, curled on her side, hands tucked in front, still bound in his shirt, eyes closed.

Kill her now. She was but a meat sack. A means for revenge.

A nobody.

A nobody like me.

He couldn't kill her while she was defenseless.

With a sigh, he sank down beside her. Close enough to have her scent in his face. Near enough he could snare her if she tried to flee.

Too far away to ever chance feeling the warmth of another person ever again.

CHAPTER FIVE

Jayda barely dared breathe when the lionman lay beside her. She'd sought to make herself appear benign. And it worked.

He settled down, not as much the savage as expected.

When her father and Adrian had spoken of this Marcus, they'd argued about his mental state.

"He's an animal," Adrian insisted. *"You can't think to reason with him."*

"I disagree. The man is still inside." Daddy *wasn't one to give up on supposed lost causes.*

"Why not just tranquilize his ass and drag him in to find out?" Jayda asked in between the nonchalant filing of her nails. It had been a long time since her last visit to the clinic, and it intrigued to see the change in Dr. Adrian Chimera. What happened to

his motto of leave no genetically modified beast behind? It was Adrian who'd first insisted there were no failures. Who refused to put any of them down.

And now, he was advocating they kill a project?

"The problem with using tranquilizing agents is, how much? A normal dose won't even make him blink. Too strong and he'll be a corpse." Daddy's concern being the safety of his patient.

The big ol' boss had other issues. "Good luck getting the guards to agree to go into the woods with anything less than a full magazine of bullets."

"Going into the woods is a bad idea. That's his turf. You need to draw this Marcus out where you can control the situation," Jayda observed.

"And how do you propose we draw him?" Adrian asked. "And before you suggest dangling yourself as bait, your dad already offered, and I said no."

"Not up to you," she stated, crossing her legs and planting her feet on the edge of his desk. She knew it would annoy him. Adrian liked things tidy.

"Yes, it is up to me. This is my clinic. My patient. My rules."

She leaned forward. "Your patient is running amok and needs to be taken in."

"Taken in to do what?" Adrian threw up his hands. "The man has regressed to an animal state."

"We've brought some back from the brink before," her daddy said.

"A handful of times. How many others have we lost?" It surprised her to hear the regret in his tone.

When had Adrian started to care?

Pussy.

"While you two argue a little longer, I'm going for a shower," she stated. A lie. She was going outside to make her own evaluation of the situation. Unlike the trigger-happy guards and screaming nurses, Jayda wasn't prone to panic and could take care of herself.

For her daddy, she'd try and see if the escaped patient could be brought back alive.

Which was why she found herself in a cave with a feral man, tawny gold like a lion, his hair an unkempt mane, and body muscled. Thickly muscled all over.

Just the way she liked her men.

Except this one was barely a man. He might be speaking to her, but the wild glinted in his gaze. The beast within burred his words. While he hadn't quite gone entirely feral, he teetered on the edge, which meant he needed to be taken care of.

Despite him crushing her phone, he'd not actually frisked Jayda. Her watch counted down and had been counting since she'd sent a single message to her father.

Coordinates, actually. But she wasn't about to wait for backup to arrive. With him calm, now was her chance.

Keeping an eye on his back, Jayda ran her hand down to her ankle, the wound-up shirt binding her wrists easy to slip free from. Marcus had turned away from her, kind of insulting really the way he treated her as a non-threat. Jayda hated it when boys treated her like a plain ol' girl.

Despite his even breathing, he stiffened. Not asleep after all. She clenched her fist around the object she'd snared and tucked it quickly into the shirt. Just in time, as he suddenly rolled from her and sprang to his feet.

"What's wrong?" She faked a groggy voice.

"Go to sleep."

"Why aren't you sleeping?"

"I must watch."

"Can you see in the dark?" she asked, rising to her knees then her feet, spotting the odd green glow of his eyes.

"I see well enough."

"You are rather interesting, lionman. You see in the dark. Speak actual words and you obviously think."

"And?"

"It just goes to show you're saner than you let

on." A creature that could think and form coherent ideas obviously had reasons for its actions. "Why did you come back?" Because she knew the question bothered not only Adrian but her father, too.

"Revenge." The gleam of his teeth was meant to intimidate. She'd seen worse in the clinic cells.

"Revenge will get you killed. You're outnumbered by guards with guns."

"Only fools rush in."

She snorted. "Only a suicidal idiot would think they could take the clinic by themselves."

"It might take some whittling, but I will have my vengeance."

"Now you're talking like a crazy person. Picking people off one by one will take forever, especially since, after the first few, your opportunities will grow scarce. They're already scared of you."

"Good." There was grim satisfaction in that single word.

It only increased his appeal.

"You know they'll just replace anyone you kill."

"Then I'll kill the new ones, too!"

She rolled her eyes. "For a guy who claims he doesn't want to be a monster, you seem determined to become one."

"Not me. Them! They made me like this." He pounded his chest.

"The doctors remade your body, but your mind is still your own," she insisted.

"No, it's not," he grumbled.

"If it's not, then you need to learn to control it." Jayda learned at a young age that control was key; in her actions, her life, her emotions. She used to be sniveling brat, who sobbed each time daddy dropped her off at boarding school. Then she grew some armor. Little touched her now.

"I can't control it. It makes me do things..." His voice dropped to a low murmur.

"Think again, lionman. You're the one acting out."

"Am not."

"Funny, because I only see one guy here, the same one who tossed me over his shoulder like a sack of potatoes. There are people who can help you with your behavior if you return to the clinic."

"No!" He roared at her. Snarled a bit, too, and stomped his feet.

She waited until he was done. "And there you go having a fit again. I'm surprised you're not on the floor kicking and screaming."

He gaped at her. "I am not a child."

"Yet you're having a tantrum instead of reasoning this through like an adult."

His gaze narrowed into a dangerous glowing slit. "Stop talking."

"Why? Are you finding it painful to realize just how far you've let yourself go?"

"As if I had a choice." He glanced down at himself. "It's not like there's showering amenities out in the woods."

"You're right. There's not, which begs the question, why stay here?" She gestured to the barren cave.

"I live here."

"We both know your real home isn't supposed to be a cave." A firm reminder.

"I have no home." There was a stark truth to his statement.

Sympathy welled in her because she knew what it felt like to have nowhere to go. No one to truly care. Daddy tried, but he wasn't very good at emotional connections. Then again, neither was she.

"The clinic can be your home."

"No." He practically shouted the word, his feet scuffing as he paced.

"They want to help you."

"I don't want their help. I've had their help." He seethed.

"So you'd rather be a lionman forever?" An intentional taunt as she stepped toward him.

"No. I'm not a lionman or a monster. I'm..." He paused. "I am Marcus."

So he did recall his name. Not as feral as Adrian thought. She gave him a slight smile. "Nice to meet you, Marcus. Do you remember my name?"

"Don't care," he grumbled as she moved even closer, close enough that the slightest sway of her body would bring her against him.

He swallowed hard as she leaned near.

She purred against the lobe of his ear, feeling his tenseness. "My name is Jayda, and you should care because that's the name of the girl taking down your ass," she whispered against his ear before jabbing him with a needle!

CHAPTER SIX

THE PROBLEM WITH INJECTING A TESTOSTERONE-hopped-up beastman? Sometimes one dose wasn't enough.

The lionman roared—literally—a loud, booming sound of rage. He heaved his body, thrusting Jayda from him. A move she had expected, which was why she rolled away into a crouch. Watching the green glow of his eyes, she pulled the second syringe free from where it was stitched inside the ankle of her pants. A part of the seam, he'd never noticed it. Hopefully it was enough. She'd lost her third sedative in the surprise of his very first attack.

He growled, a low menacing grumble. "You tricked me."

"I did. Silly, kitty." She smiled, knowing he saw the white pearliness even in the dark.

"You work for them."

"Work. Volunteer. Daddy calls for help, and as a good little girl, I go running." She ignored the part of her that claimed she still sought daddy's approval.

"You were sent to fetch me?" He sounded quite incredulous.

She smirked. "Did you really think no one noticed you? As to fetch? I can also kill." She rolled her shoulders. "The choice is kind of up to you."

"I'll kill you first."

"Go ahead and try. Already you're getting slower."

"What's in the needle?" he asked, blinking his eyes and shuffling to his left.

She kept him in sight. "You might as well give in. I've got you beat. I injected you with enough Special K to put down an elephant." The big man in front of her might not come close to the weight, but with his potential adrenaline and heightened ability to metabolize drugs, they needed large doses. Problem was figuring out how much was too much.

"Not going back." The statement emerged guttural. His eyes dipped as he crouched and slowly shifted to the right. She kept pace and watched him. He'd make a move at one point. She had to be ready.

"My daddy can help you." After all, he'd given Jayda a new lease on life and since then paid her more attention than he had her entire childhood. Because she was finally interesting to him.

Funny how once she got what she always wanted, she was the one to walk away.

"I've seen what his help looks like." His lower lip curled.

"Which is why you need to go back. It has to be tweaked. Sometimes the process isn't perfect. It needs to be helped along."

"More drugs?" He snorted. "No thanks."

"Got a better idea?"

"You talk too much. Should have killed you." He bared his teeth, still showing no signs of lethargy.

Dammit.

"Ah, kitty, now that ain't nice. Here I thought we were becoming friends."

"Not friends."

"You're right, probably better that way. You'll be less pissed when I put you to sleep."

"I said no more drugs." He lunged at her, and she didn't quite dodge so much as embrace him, letting his weight and momentum drive into her. He slammed them into the wall hard enough her breath caught. Her body tensed as he leaned into her. Close to three hundred pounds of man. Muscle.

And heat.

So much heat...

One of her hands ended up on the bare skin of his torso. A sizzle. A sucked-in breath.

By them both.

Their eyes locked, his glowing gaze captivating. The moment still. Silent. The perfect chance to slam the other needle in and push the plunger home.

The expression in his eyes shifted. Surprise, a touch of fear, followed by anger.

But it was her emotions that surprised her most of all.

Intrigue and arousal.

Both of which peaked when he went limp against her, but not before whispering, "Only beauty can fell the beast."

What did that mean?

Jayda couldn't ask. He slumped, the second dose of the drugs dropping him finally. Even prone on the ground, he kept an aura of menace. So much strength in that body. Danger.

Yet gentleness, too. In all their interactions thus far, he'd not harmed her. Not even a tiny bruise. Even when he'd slammed her against the wall, she was cushioned by his hands, his body taking the brunt.

However, she couldn't count on that forever. She'd read the report. Once projects went feral, they didn't hesitate to kill, which meant if they didn't want a casualty they needed to move him. Fast!

Heading to the mouth of the cave, she quickly tapped her heel, the compartment popping open to give her a needle-thin flare. Cracking it first, she tossed it at the rock in front of the slit. Night had fallen. The drones her father had patrolling the sky would quickly spot it and dispatch men to find her.

Having marked the area, she headed back to the cave and heaved—with much cursing of his luscious largeness—the rather unwieldy Marcus through the narrow slit. Leaving him in a heap by the lip of his cave, she paused, listening.

In the distance, she perceived a whine that grew louder and turned into the rev of engines. A pair of all-terrain vehicles shot out of the woods with a fierce whiiiiiing of sound.

Not discreet at all.

She eyed Marcus and noted he still slept. But that didn't mean the cacophony wouldn't wake him. Waving her hand, she skipped down the rocks and flagged down a driver.

He was going to talk, so she gave him a look that shut him up on "Hey."

She snared the cuffs dangling from his belt and headed back up the rocky outcrop.

The metal bracelets might not do much to slow

down the lionman, but even a second might make a difference if he woke during transport.

The guys on the noisy rigs eyed Marcus askance, waiting for the final machine to arrive. Larger than the pair of ATVs, it had a cargo area. It took two of them—grunting and heaving—to lift his body. Jayda didn't even try to hide her smirk.

Pussies.

Literally. Having spent an hour in the gym earlier with some of them, she knew what they *weren't* capable of. Add to that the idiots thought it was hot she could bend them into a pretzel. She, on the other hand, wasn't as impressed.

She liked her men big and strong. Able to handle a little roughness.

Her gaze strayed to the lionman strapped in the back of the full-sized ATV. He'd be pissed when he woke.

She tapped one of the riders of the smaller machines on the shoulder. "You ride with him." She jerked toward the passenger side of the transport. "I'm taking your machine."

The guard knew better than to argue, but that didn't mean he looked pleased about it. She leaned in close to his cheek and whispered, "Keep in mind he's more valuable than you are. Which is why I'll be taking this." She lifted the gun from his holster and tucked it in the back of her pants.

When he lunged with a snapped, "Bitch, give that back," she lifted a hand and shoved him in the chest.

The guard stumbled, and she said very softly, "I wouldn't suggest doing that again." She'd killed for less.

One of the idiot's buddies chose to walk by and slap him. "Let's go before he wakes up."

A wise plan. But they needn't have worried. The lion slept all the way to the clinic, where her father oversaw his transport to six level. The deepest ward for the more difficult patients.

She kept her tone and expression dispassionate as he was loaded onto a heavy-duty hospital bed. Thick metal bands were placed around his chest. Wrists. Ankles. Even his neck was restrained.

So dangerous.

Which was why she had to walk away, telling her father, "I'm going to wrangle some food." And maybe see if she could find a guard who wouldn't break—or cry—if she took him to bed.

She needed something to ease the pressure before she did something her daddy wouldn't like.

47

CHAPTER SEVEN

THE HEADACHE THROBBED IN HIS BROW. A DEEP, aching thud of pain, utterly familiar. Which made it disturbing.

The sedatives given by the doctors always made him feel like shit.

His tongue sat thick and pasty inside his mouth. Gravity hated his body. Marcus couldn't move it. At all. Not even if he wanted to, given the restraints holding him down.

I'm not in my cave anymore.

Because he'd been betrayed by a woman.

He should have known better.

Should have killed her.

But how could he when he found himself pressing against her, her body cradled in his arms.

The feel of her plush and shapely, her gaze unafraid. Bold and sexy.

Even now he couldn't hate her. Lust, though... What he wouldn't give to have her in reach again.

I won't be touching anyone for a while. Because he'd stupidly gotten caught.

Marcus opened his gritty eyes to a ceiling made of concrete, the lights within it recessed. Nothing to grab should a patient get free. Which would be difficult, given the bands on the bed had been reinforced. Thick metal that didn't budge when he pulled at first one wrist then the other.

A prisoner because of a woman. The fact he'd so misjudged her should have rankled. Yet, there was a certain admiration in him at her courage.

Who went toe to toe with a monster? Was that why he was loath to hurt her? Why he let her stab him?

Or perhaps, there was a more insidious reason for his capture.

I wanted to come back.

For a while he'd been roaming the outskirts of the clinic, wondering at his return, the purpose for it. He'd assumed it was for revenge. Yet, if that were the case, why hadn't he killed anyone? All he did was watch. Biding his time because, subconsciously perhaps, he wanted the doctors to do something.

Anything. Because if they didn't help him, then the human known as Marcus would cease to exist.

How could I volunteer for this? Probably on account that Jayda was right when she said he'd die. He couldn't live in the woods forever.

A scrape of a shoe snapped his attention to the left, to a spot just over his shoulder. A blind spot he couldn't see, yet he recognized the scent. Irish Spring soap. Clean, crisp, and only used by one man.

"You're awake. Excellent. I was getting worried the second dose she gave you might have been too much." Dr. Cerberus, with a voice smooth as an announcer on a drowsy four a.m. radio show, preceded the man.

The bed Marcus lay upon tilted, machinery whirring to life and lifting him to an upright position. It had the benefit of making him tower over Cerberus. All the better to scowl.

Marcus showed teeth as he said, "I'm going to eat your heart in front of you."

The doctor clapped his hands and smiled. "You can speak! I knew you still had your mind. This is marvelous news. It means there is a way to push back the feral nature of the cure."

"Don't you mean curse?" Marcus curled his lip. "And who says I'm not a savage?"

"You do seem rather untamed compared to

previous times, but that is probably a result of your lack of socialization in the wild."

"Never claimed I was alone." He wasn't the only one to have escaped. Also not the first to return and get caught.

"Really?" Cerberus sounded pleased. "We theorized you might have congregated outside of the clinic. You'll have to tell us all about your adventure."

At the statement, Marcus clamped his lips tight.

"Don't be quiet on my account. Jayda told me you were quite coherent in the cave."

Jayda, the name of the one who'd brought him down. A beautiful maiden to tempt the beast.

He couldn't stay silent. "I should have killed her."

"But you didn't because you've not completely gone over the edge."

"Haven't I?" Because he certainly didn't feel like himself anymore.

"Your treatment of Jayda proves it. I knew she'd draw you out." Cerberus appeared so smug.

Whereas Marcus felt surprise. "You used your own kid against me?"

Cerberus didn't seem daunted by the fact he'd put her in danger. "Who better to make sure my orders were followed? Do you know many others would have simply put you down like a dog?" Cerberus shook his head as he headed for a sink to wash his hands. "I wanted you alive."

"Alive to run more tests." Marcus sneered. "How many will it take to realize you failed?"

"Have we?" Cerberus turned from the sink, definitely looking younger than ever. And was that a fiery red glint in his eye?

"Unbelievable," Marcus muttered. No denying what the doctor had done.

"What is unbelievable is the fact you still protest the results."

"Have you looked at me?" The face in the mirror was not the man he knew. Marcus, before everything happened, had weighed a hundred and fifty pounds soaking wet. Stood a skinny five feet seven. Thin hair on top, looking at going bald by thirty. Skin pock-marked by rough teen years rife with acne. Now he was well over six feet, thickly muscled with hair ridiculously thick. His skin was clear, of not only blemishes but scars too.

"I see a man in his prime. Excellent physique. Younger than his almost forty years."

A handsome guy if you liked them thick and hairy. "Problem is I'm no longer a man." No longer himself.

"Are you sure of that?" Cerberus riposted. "You

sound like one, full of doubts and thoughts. Not an animal in the least."

Now perhaps. But a few days ago... He remembered running on all fours in the woods, intent on chasing a rabbit. Eager to catch it. Feel the hot juices as he chomped.

"Trust me when I say the monster lurks not far." The lucidity was but a short relapse.

"You're not a monster. You need to see your abilities more like a new limb that needs to be trained in proper use."

"Trained?" Marcus snorted. "How exactly am I supposed to train when I'm a prisoner?"

"Show yourself to be civil and maybe you'll earn some freedom."

"I'll be civil only if you keep your needles and piss cups away." He eyed the uncapped needle in Cerberus's hand.

"We need to see what's going on in your body," Cerberus exclaimed, pressing the tip of the needle against clean skin.

His washed skin. He'd slept long enough they'd even managed to bathe him. He wore clean white scrubs and a sheet tucked tightly around his hips.

"No." He bucked in the restraints, roaring as the needle poked and took what it wanted.

And he could do nothing about it.

The beast in him rose, roaring and pushing. Snarling loud enough that Cerberus stepped back, only to grab another syringe and wag it. "Don't make me put you to sleep."

"Let me go!" A useless demand.

"If you cooperated, this wouldn't be necessary." That prick Cerberus sounded so fucking prissy saying it.

"Cooperating made me into a monster."

"Hardly a monster."

"Your daughter called me a lionman."

"Apt enough even though you have more than just feline DNA meshed with yours."

"Monster science," he spat.

"Revolutionary medicine," Cerberus corrected. "With astonishing results. You seem to have forgotten what life was like before." A reminder of the car accident that had left him broken and in a coma. Hooked to machines. No better than a vegetable. The clinic made an offer to the hospital to care for him, for free. Or so they told him once he woke up.

Perhaps if he'd experienced the horror of his almost-dead body he'd have a better appreciation.

But he didn't. "Better dead than becoming something else."

"Only if you let it control you. Mind over matter," Cerberus stated, tapping his temple.

"Is that what you keep telling yourself?" His words turned sly. "You've taken some of the supposed miracle cure. You think it's doing good. You're looking younger. Fit. Maybe your cock is finally working again without a little pill. But inside, it's changing you. Twisting your thoughts. Fucking with your needs. You'll see. Soon you won't be you anymore."

"You're right. I won't. I'll be something better." Cerberus pressed the button that put Marcus in a sleeping position again.

Then left.

The next time Marcus saw him, he refused to talk. Wouldn't eat. Spent his time roaring and pulling. Hoping each time he strained that something would break.

Something did. His mind snapped.

CHAPTER EIGHT

"WHAT'S WRONG WITH HIM?" JAYDA ASKED staring at a video monitor with the channel set on Marcus' room.

It had been five days since they'd captured the lionman, and she'd yet to leave. The first day was because the helicopter needed repair. Then there was a sighting of a project in the woods that took a few days to hunt. Now a late fall thunderstorm kept the chopper grounded.

But most of all, she just didn't want to leave. Felt almost compelled to stay. Which made no sense. Jayda didn't even like the clinic. She only showed up because her father was here. She spent most of her time, when she wasn't working, at her home in South America where it was warm.

She should be there right now, and yet instead,

she'd just finished her second jog of the day. Boredom made her exercise. It also was a wakeup call. Time to go. The moment the weather lifted, she would fly out of here.

First, though, she tracked down her father who'd been working quite a bit since she'd captured the lionman. Her daddy wouldn't say much about the project other than he was fascinating.

She totally agreed, hence why she'd spent the last few days not going anywhere near him.

But having decided she would be leaving, possibly within a few hours, she thought, why not pop in for a peek?

What she saw shocked on the screen. The lionman looked more feral than ever. As well as gaunt.

"What's wrong with him?" she asked, noticing the tubes running into his body.

"He's been degrading health-wise since we got him," her father said, barely paying her any mind. Story of her life.

"Meaning?"

"He won't eat. The nutrients we're feeding him aren't making a difference. He's stopped speaking."

"Giving you the silent treatment?" She'd done that a time or two in her youth. Problem was Daddy never actually noticed.

Her dad shook his head. "More like he doesn't know how. He's reverted back to a more primal state. We're not even able to get single words from him, let alone anything strung into a sentence."

"Did you treat him with more of the serum?" Had they pushed him over the edge where the animal genes coursing within outnumbered the man?

"No," her father sputtered, his frustration clear. "He's been given nothing but food."

Jayda stared at the screen, the vibrant man from the cave a limp, emaciated version of himself. It bothered her to see him brought so low.

"He's dying." Willing himself to die or unable to survive as a prisoner, either way, the result was the same.

"He is."

For some reason, she blurted out, "Stop it."

"I wish I could. We've tried everything." Her father shrugged. "I don't know what else to do."

"There has to be something. Have you zapped him?"

Clear reproach shone in her father's gaze. "Despite your belief, we've never zapped anybody."

No, just blended their genomes with a cocktail of beasts.

"Have you talked to him? Maybe he's feeling lonely."

"I've been in daily to speak with him. As has Adrian, even other staff. He's not responded to anyone unless it's to snap his teeth or growl."

A crease formed in her forehead. "You said he won't eat. What have you tried giving him? Did you ensure he had some fresh raw meat?" Because if he'd turned feral, cooked and processed foods might not appeal.

"We've tried everything. From fruits and vegetables to starches and carbs. Rare steak. Ice cream. Yesterday, we even tried dangling a live turkey in front of his face. And nada." Daddy shook his head.

"You can't expect him to attack something while he's bound." She goggled her father. "Untie him. Give him some freedom to move."

"We tried that already." Her father's lips compressed.

"What happened?"

"He almost killed himself bashing his head on the wall."

"Oh shit."

"We had to flood the room with gas to knock him out and get him back in the bed."

"There must be something we can try," Jayda mused aloud. She couldn't help but remember the man in the cave. The bitterness in his voice. Angry because he felt betrayed. Seeking revenge, which gave him focus.

Emotion was what had driven him before.

Her father left to do his rounds of the other projects, and Jayda spent a moment staring at Marcus. He lay prone, eyes open and staring. Unseeing. Almost dead.

Totally unacceptable.

Before she could think twice, she was in the room with Marcus. She tapped his scruffy chin. "Wakey, wakey, kitty."

He didn't twitch, didn't even blink those staring eyes, yet she noted a slight hitch in his breathing.

She leaned forward. "I can't believe you're being such a coward."

His breath stopped.

"Giving up. I didn't take you for a suck-ass pussy." Said with all the disdain she could muster.

It worked.

He fixed her with a dark gaze, the green light in his eyes dull. "Arrggggggr."

"What's that?" She cupped a hand to her ear. "I can't understand on account you're talking monster."

A tiny prick of light lit within his pupil. "Gggggggg."

"Still not catching it, kitty. If you want to say

something, spit it out." She stared at him, noting the light in his eyes getting steadier.

"Gggo."

"One syllable? It's a start. But you'll have to do better than that if you want me to leave."

"Go. A. Way." Each word separate and slow.

She leaned closer, noticing the golden, furred line of his jaw, the scent of him, clean, yet still hinting of musk. She inhaled and moved even closer.

"I ain't leaving yet, kitty. Matter of fact, I might stick around for a while."

"Go away." This time the demand had an imperious tone to it. The clarity in his eyes brightened.

Pleasure unfurled within her as he responded. "Don't tell me you're still sore I bested you."

"Tricked me," he huffed.

"I did." Said with a smile. Jayda turned from him and moved to the back of the table, knowing it would drive him a little nuts. "Little ol' me bested the big bad kitty."

"Drugged me. Not fair." A hint of petulance in the words, and he was becoming more and more coherent. Responding to human interaction, which begged the question, was daddy just not feeding him enough mentally?

She circled back to the front and stood before Marcus, hands on the hips of her black jeans, her hair loose over her shoulders. He might still be lying down, but he craned to keep her in sight.

"Are you demanding a rematch, kitty?"

"Let me loose." No mistaking the sensual grin on his lips.

It wasn't the lips on her face that loosened in reply. She crossed her arms and cocked her head. "You know, I'm tempted to do that, kitty. But those silly guards, they'd probably come running in here and panic. I'd hate for them to shoot me when they're trying to put you down."

"Bad aim."

She couldn't stop the deep chuckle. "Bad aim, indeed. I hear you're not eating."

"Not hungry." Grumbled with a scowl.

"Not talking either."

He shrugged. "Nothing to say."

"Yet you're talking to me."

"Because you won't go away." Said with a hint of exasperation, something she specialized at.

"I would, but the helicopter is broken," she lied. "Could take a while to get the new part."

"Go wait somewhere else. I don't want to talk to you." He spoke with a gruff undertone but was completely understandable.

"Then stop talking, kitty." She leaned close. "Or are you going to admit you like chatting with me?

Does the big bad lionman have a thing for chocolate honey?"

He sucked in a breath. "Not attracted."

"So if I put my hand on your cock, it won't say hello?" she purred. Her gaze dropped to the spot below his waist. The sheet definitely tented.

"That's abuse."

"Only if you don't give me permission." She cast him a sly glance. "Tell me to touch you, kitty."

"Stop it." Hissed at her, yet his eyes blazed, and the heat of him warmed the space between them.

"Do you really want me to stop, kitty? Or would you rather I touch you? Because I'll bet it's been a long time since a woman touched you. And teased you." She stepped closer and held her hand not even an inch from him. He stiffened. All over.

"This is cruel." The tone was broken.

"I keep offering to put you out of your misery." She leaned close that enough her hair dangled to hide them. Her lips were close enough for her breath to touch his. "Do you want me to touch you, kitty?"

"I..." He said no more, only stared.

It was enough to ignite a pulse between her legs. To bring her close enough she could—

"Jayda!" The single word barked through the speaker in the ceiling, ruining the moment, halting her actions.

She withdrew with a sigh.

"You are being paged." His gaze flicked to the speaker high overhead.

"Just my daddy. He can wait. We weren't done." She trailed a finger up his arm, dancing over the thin fabric, noticing the fine tremor in his flesh.

"What do you want from me?"

"I suppose just sex where you don't talk is out of the question?"

"You're incredible." Muttered with a slight shake of his head.

"Oh, I am," she said with a husky chuckle. "Wait until you feel—"

"Jayda, that's quite enough!" her daddy yelled.

"Cerberus is mad," Marcus observed.

"More like being overprotective a little too late." She rolled her eyes. "Guess we'll have to finish this later, kitty."

"No later. You need to leave and don't come back."

"You're not in a position to demand," she retorted. And why wasn't he jumping at what she offered? She could tell he desired her. So why refuse?

"I don't want to see you."

"And I don't want to listen to my father lecture

me about playing with his pets. But we can't always get what we want."

He clamped his lips.

"Are you gonna say goodbye, kitty?"

He closed his eyes and remained silent.

"Ooh, look at you faking it. It won't work. Daddy knows, and once I leave, you'll have to deal with those other morons."

Not one word spoken and yet she could have sworn she heard him say, *Fuck anyone else.*

She patted him on the cheek. "I'm with you on that, kitty. Fuck the world."

Before she could give in to the temptation to stay —which tugged at her more than it should have—she exited the wing housing Marcus and ran into her dad. "Before you start freaking out, sorry I visited your lionman. I know you hate it when I do that." Mostly on account she had a tendency of riling up the patients with her mere presence.

To her surprise, her father beamed. "Actually, I'm glad you did. That's the most coherent he's been since his arrival. You managed to snap him out of his funk. Which is why Adrian is about to enlist your aid."

"Aid doing what? I thought we took care of all the projects in the wood."

"I'm talking about Marcus."

"What about him?" She played dumb. "You don't need me since he's already locked up. Now that you know he's faking, I'm sure you can handle him."

"Except I don't think he was faking for us. He only appears to respond to you."

Again, a spurt of pleasure followed by a deep cold as a chain of obligation wound around her freedom. "I'm sure that's just a coincidence. And even if it's not, I'm supposed to leave. I've got business to attend." A job in South America then a pleasure spree in France that would end in tragedy—for others.

"They'll have to wait. You're needed here."

Not *I need you.* With Daddy, some things never changed. Business first. And family...well, family was there to help business.

But she wasn't a malleable little girl anymore. She had her own needs and wishes. She wasn't about to let them dictate her actions. So why the fuck did she say, "I can probably give it a few more days."

A few days to screw around with lionman, possibly quite nakedly, to get that urge out of her system. Get him talking to her daddy again, and then she'd leave.

And maybe this time she'd stay away instead of getting drawn back over and over again to this place —where she was reborn.

CHAPTER NINE

IMPATIENCE THRUMMED INSIDE ADRIAN AS HE waited, hands tucked behind his back, for Cerberus to arrive at his office with his daughter. He'd demanded their presence the moment he saw the transformation in Marcus.

But how to convince the woman to stay?

Knowing Aloysius, he'd already broached Jayda with the subject of staying longer. Knowing Jayda, she'd bitched and moaned. Possibly needed to be coaxed with money. But while she might negotiate hard, she would stay. Adrian would make sure of that. A few days at least, which might be all that was needed.

Watching Jayda talking to Marcus, actually chatting, had given him an idea. A theory that might explain some anomalies in his research.

The biggest issue Adrian ran into with his cure was the humanity—and in some cases sanity—of the subjects. It started not long after the physical changes. The projects each experienced it differently. Some claimed to hear voices in their heads. Others experienced drastic mood swings. Primal urges, especially those of the hunt, rose and pounded through the veins.

The allure of the wild could take over. Actually had in a few cases. But a few managed to come back from the brink. To find their way, so to speak. Like Luke. A project kept locked up for his and everyone else's safety until the day he met a certain nurse. The failure that used to haunt Adrian now gave him hope, because if Luke could rein in his baser impulses, then surely others could, too.

All it took in Luke's case was falling in love.

What if, and this was revolutionary thinking, the test subjects needed a partner to remain grounded? Perhaps there was something in the air between the attracted pair, some chemical reaction that calmed the inner beast.

Adrian wanted to study the possibility. Problem being thus far he only had a few examples to draw from. Luke and Nurse Margaret would have made fine test subjects, but they went missing somewhere in a South American jungle. There was Becky and

Jett, still at the clinic. The only thing was Becky never lost her mind, just her ability to breathe air twice a month. A fascinating thing on its own.

There was his colleague, Doctor Jackal, who ran off with a patient named Geoffrey. The lovers had taken up open residence in Paris. Almost daring Adrian to send someone after them.

Yet, he didn't. He watched them instead. Because Geoffrey, once upon a time, was thought to be too far-gone. Then Jackal began treating him. Not with drugs but by his mere presence.

Perhaps it wasn't love but pheromones? A chemical reaction caused by the mixing of certain scents.

He needed to test his theory further. Take samples. Set some baseline tests. Marcus and his response to Jayda presented the perfect opportunity.

Test all you want, boyo. You're screwed. There is no one for you. Just a slow descent into madness.

The thing he feared most.

The moment Aloysius entered with his daughter, Adrian clapped his hands. "About time the pair of you got here."

"Blame your slow elevator. Whose idea was it to build only one of those again?"

There were actually two, but the other one was kept hidden and exclusive for his use.

"The stairs provide an excellent form of cardio. I

69

recommend doing the entire building, all of the levels, at least twice a day." Adrian didn't use the public staircase, of course. He ran the steps out of sight lest anyone see the demons riding his flesh. He needed to expunge them several times a day.

For how much longer would he be able to outrun them? And if he lost his mind, what would happen to—

"I brought her," Aloysius interrupted. "Tell her what you want to do."

Adrian canted his head. "As if you didn't already broach it."

"All he said was you wanted me to stay to help you with Marcus." Jayda took her usual spot, legs hooked over the arm of the chair.

"Is that all you told her?" Adrian shot Aloysius a look. "There was discussion of other options."

"Such as?" she asked. "Because if I don't have to stay..."

"Personally, I think we should eliminate the failure and learn from our mistakes." Adrian tossed his suggestion out and watched her reaction.

Aloysius barked first. "Already said I am not agreeing to an autopsy."

"What? Autopsy on who?" Jayda eyed them both. Understanding dawned in her gaze. "But he's not dead."

"Yet." Adrian shrugged. "But let's be honest, he's not thriving in our care. So it won't be long."

"Dad said you thought I might be able to help with him."

She didn't quite offer, which was why Adrian turned her down. "A few days won't do us much good. If he only responds to you, then the moment you leave we'll be back to square one."

"If he responds," Jayda repeated. "Could be I just caught him on a good day. Maybe you should try having more visitors, more people interacting."

Adrian arched a brow. "What makes you think we haven't?"

Jumping in, Aloysius enumerated their efforts. "We've had three different nurses caring for him, eight-hour shifts. Apart from myself and Adrian, Dr. Hathor also tried talking to him. She even resorted to inappropriate attire, displaying her bosoms at an advantage to entice him, to no avail."

At the claim, Jayda snorted. "You whored out Jenny? What about a hot guy? Maybe he's into dudes."

"We've had four guards try and engage him. Not so much as a twitch. Strangest thing. Which means you are probably correct. He was having a good day and you had nothing to do with it." Adrian kept lining the bait, watching Jayda as she frowned.

You just can't help yourself. Even as he regretted his actions, he kept digging that hole deeper.

"So you think he's going to go back to dying again?"

"It seems most likely."

"Surely there's something you can do? A treatment, drug..." Jayda searched for solutions, and Adrian shook his head.

"The only thing that might snap him out of it is letting him go."

"You can't do that," Cerberus shouted. "We just found him."

"And we're killing him." Adrian noted. "What's the harm in letting him live free?"

It was Jayda who had a reply. "If you're going to do that, you should order some seeds for planting, as I hear blood is a great fertilizer."

Aloysius glared at his daughter. "Not funny."

"Killing is never a joke, Daddy. Now let's be honest. Adrian isn't going to let that kitty with rage issues loose, because then he'd end up with a whack of dead people."

Aloysius rubbed at his chin. "Would he kill anyone? He didn't kill you."

"He was planning to."

"But never went through with it," Adrian added. "Do you think he really would have?"

She shrugged. "Hard to tell."

"Let me ask, do you think he can still learn control?" Because every day Adrian worried that it would be his last in charge.

Careful words emerged slowly from her. "I think he's a very angry man."

"You used to be angry," Adrian reminded her. He still remembered the teenager, never content, always screaming. Back in those days she never noticed the cripple who partnered with her father in the lab. She showed up out of control, ranting, the result of taking drugs for years, part of how she coped with an ugly parental split. She hit rock bottom and ended up in forced rehab.

Through it all, Cerberus stayed by her side, and when her use of drugs returned to haunt in the form of organ failure, he did what any father would do. Fixed his daughter. One of their most successful cases.

If the most challenging to deal with at times.

"Who says I'm not still pissed at the world?" Jayda smirked.

"You might be angry, and yet you are in control," Adrian pointed out. Just like he was in charge. Most of the time. The times he could remember. But what about the moments he couldn't? Hours lost at a time.

Jayda rolled her eyes. "It's called getting older and wiser. I've learned how to channel my rage."

"Teach him," Adrian insisted. "Teach Marcus how to not give in to the beast." He didn't tell her the rest. *Get close to the man because the closer you get, the saner he is.* If they could bring him back from the edge, then there was hope for all his patients.

Not you, boyo. You are doomed. How he wanted to throttle that inner voice.

"You want me to teach someone how to not be angry?" At that, she laughed. "I am more likely to send him on a murderous rampage. You do recall I am the one who put him back in chains."

"Then you can be the one to release him."

At Adrian's pat reply, she snorted. "I thought you wanted him alive. We both know what will happen if he gets loose and comes at me."

"Are you sure he'll try and kill you?"

Aloysius finally stepped in. "I don't know if Jayda has the right temperament to be in charge of Marcus's recovery."

"Way to call me a bitch, Daddy." Jayda seemed more amused than offended.

"You're welcome, sweetheart. Because it's the truth. I know coercing you will have an opposite effect. I think we should find someone else to entice Marcus."

"You mean another woman?" Jayda snorted. "Way to be a pimp. I'll have to order you a gold chain for Christmas."

"That's just it. I don't think anyone else will work." Adrian grabbed a remote from his desk and used it to load a video of Jayda and Marcus, showing him listless moments before her entry. His lively engagement with her. He paused it with Marcus sporting a partial smile.

"Look at him. A few hours ago, I would have said he had a few days to live. Then Jayda walks into the room, and next thing you know, his heartrate is up, he's talking, and looking like he just gotten a shot of life."

"He's horny. Send in a cute nurse," Aloysius suggested, which earned him a glare from Jayda.

"We have had cute nurses. Male and female. Ugly ones, too. Yet none got so much as a twitch." Adrian jabbed a finger at Jayda. "We need her."

"Her is standing right here, so rather than talking to my dad, try talking to me."

Adrian faced her. "Stay."

"No." She didn't hesitate. "You're nuts if you think I can help him."

"Exactly my point!" Aloysius jumped in to agree. "Jayda isn't equipped to help him."

"Excuse me?" She turned a glare on her father.

"Let me remind you that you contacted *me* for help. Not the other way around."

"To hunt him. Not play the part of therapist," Jayda's father said with exasperation. "Your part is done. Time for you to go."

"Way to kick me out."

"Then stay," Aloysius snapped.

"No, thanks. I've got better things to do." She angled her chin.

The whole thing proved disappointing but predictable. Jayda never stayed long to visit. Mostly because she and her father ended up at odds.

However, if she left, how was Adrian to prove his hypothesis?

He needed to change her mind.

Adrian waved a hand at her. "I didn't realize you had other commitments. In that case, you should go. We'll find someone else to dangle and see if Marcus bites. I'll ask Lowry to find someone young and attractive. Given his interest in you, perhaps we need a lady of tanned complexion."

Jayda's cheeks took on a hint of color. "As if you can replace me."

"We don't really have a choice since you're refusing," Adrian taunted.

"Don't listen to Adrian," Aloysius interjected. "Go. Let the pros handle Marcus."

"The pros?" Disdain in that reply. "Neither of you has the slightest clue how to handle a guy like him, or you would have already."

"And you think you know better?" More shade was thrown, and Adrian saw where Jayda got her attitude.

"Last time I saw him, he talked to me, not you."

"A fluke." Aloysius waved dismissively.

"Or not." She faced Adrian. "If I stay, I'll expect to be paid and given free rein."

Aloysius butted in. "Like hell."

"I'm sorry, but last I checked, I was well past the age of majority, Daddy." She shot him a glare. "I can do whatever I like."

"Not in this case you won't, because I know what's happening here." Aloysius lasered Adrian with his gaze. "I won't let you do it."

"Do what?" Adrian asked in all innocence.

"She's not sleeping with Marcus."

"Never asked her to," Adrian drawled.

"I can't believe you said that, Daddy." Huffed with hands on her hips.

"Because it's true. Ask him. He wants you to fornicate with his pet to further his studies." Aloysius jabbed a finger in his direction.

Jayda arched a brow. "He can want all he wants, even ask, but I'd tell him the same thing as I'll tell you. Who I screw is my decision. And if I do it with the lionman, it will be because I want it and no other reason."

"You will not sleep with Marcus!" Aloysius boomed.

"Please. I never sleep with guys. I'm a leave-them-after-sex kind of girl."

Adrian covered his mouth lest they see his grin. The antics of the father-daughter pair never ceased to amuse.

Poor Aloysius turned a mottled color, and if he wasn't taking the treatment, Adrian might have worried about his heart.

The dark-skinned doctor crossed his arms, expression mulish. "You need to leave. Tomorrow. On the first flight."

"But, Daddy, don't you want to spend time together?" She batted her lashes, and Aloysius ground his teeth. She laughed. "Lighten up. I can't believe you're freaking about lionman and me getting freaky between the sheets. Weren't you the one all giddy about some of the staff and pets fucking and making monster babies?"

"They're not monsters," Adrian defended. Mostly. Although nurse Becky had some interesting things happening in her tummy.

"I am interested in it happening to other people.

Not my daughter. You're not staying here. Not having sex with any of the projects. Most definitely *not* getting pregnant," Aloysius declared. "I forbid it."

Jayda held her father's stare for a moment before laughing. She laughed so hard she wiped tears from her eyes. "Holy fuck, that was priceless. Forbidding me." She snorted. "Just so you know, I'm staying, but if it makes you feel any better, I'm not going to screw your pet kitty. Mostly because I am not keen on cameras watching my every move. But I will see if I can teach him to play nice."

"Promise?" Aloysius almost pled.

"You know I live to break promises, Daddy. But don't worry, I'll try and remember a condom if I do." She winked and then left.

Adrian waited to be sure she was gone before saying, "You do realize, by forbidding her, she's probably going to—"

"Have sex with him? I should hope so. Can you imagine the children they might have?" Aloysius rubbed his hands, completely enthused.

That was cold even by Adrian's standards.

What was happening to him? To his mind? What before Adrian had done with impunity, now began to bother. Was it a symptom of his cure?

Or a sign of his descent into madness?

CHAPTER TEN

MARCUS DID HIS BEST TO SINK BACK INTO apathy. A more difficult task than expected after Jayda's last visit. She left him agitated. Questioning. Wondering if he truly wanted to give up.

He'd thought himself decided. It became clear not long after his arrival that the doctors couldn't save him from the madness overtaking him. He could feel himself, the man, slipping away, bit by bit.

Then she appeared, expression sassy, her words a challenge. Daring him to fight. Waking him in a way that belied reason. The allure that had pulled him from the forest once again yanked him from his stupor.

It seemed all she had to do was walk into a room and all his senses went into high gear. Even after she left, the lingering scent of her, the *feel* of her, remained. Tantalizing...

It took a reminder that she probably wouldn't return for him to finally calm himself. To close his eyes and drop into a serene state that his more bestial side didn't appreciate at all. *It* wanted to fight.

It didn't realize just how hopeless it was.

Marcus never learned. He still remembered the first time he woke up.

His whole body felt heavy. Like the morning after a night of gaming and too many caffeine drinks to stay awake. A nerd's version of a hangover. Except he woke in a place with a strange smell. A hospital-like scent of bleach, and something else.

Something that wrinkled his nose.

He opened his eyes to see a light overhead. Not his bedroom light. Not his room, he realized, looking to the side. The machines were strange in appearance. Full of lights and humming. Without his glasses, they seemed quite alien, which might be why he hyperventilated and sat up.

Where am I? *He pushed to remember. What was the last thing...He recalled getting ready to start a marathon online war event. Which meant stocking up on treats. He was crossing the road, against the light, in a hurry to make it home when—*

He whimpered at the sudden recollection of impact. And pain. Then nothing. Pure nothing.

Because aliens kidnapped me! *The only answer.*

He swung his legs off the bed and ignored the voice that said, "Please remain lying down."

As if he'd listen to his alien abductors. The sheet slipped from him, leaving him nude with only tubes running into his body. Into his... He squealed at the sight of the catheter in his penis.

Yanking it only caused pain, which might have been why he reacted how he did when the door opened and a woman appeared in a white blouse and a ridiculous cap with a red cross.

He roared and lashed out.

Which led to him waking up in a different bed. Still in a cell. Not hooked to machines but a prisoner. And when he asked why, the stupid answer they gave, "You're helping to save humanity."

Ironic, because they were the reason he lost his.

Yet he'd returned to the clinic, lured by a temptress, and now trapped in a nightmare with no escape.

Nothing to look forward to. Not even a glimpse of Jayda, who'd left and probably wouldn't return.

Which was for the best. He didn't want the only woman who could somehow manage to rouse him from apathy around. Everyone else he could ignore.

And he did. The evening nurse came to check on him. He feigned sleep. A guard checked in. His breathing remained steady.

Another nurse around dinnertime wasn't worth a sniff.

He slumbered for real until the door opened again a short while later, which, in and of itself, he could have ignored. Technicians bustled in and out all the time. Cerberus and Adrian loved to visit, too. Those he took special pleasure in disregarding.

But the scent that hit him, the awareness that raised every single hair on his body—and he had a lot of hair—told him who entered. Who actually returned to torture him.

He refused to look. Didn't twitch a single muscle. She moved silently, which was why it surprised him to suddenly hear the hum of machinery and the jolt as the bed went into motion, tilting him upright.

Even once it stopped, he kept his eyes shut. Didn't move a muscle at all. Didn't hear a thing other than the whoosh and hum of the machines trying to keep him alive.

Felt...her warm breath on his lips, which caused him to suddenly stare. She grinned at him, taller than expected given she looked him in the eye. A glance down showed her feet dangled because she held herself off the floor using the rails on the bed to suspend herself.

A display of easy strength. And he liked it. Liked it a hell of a lot.

She kept his gaze for a moment before she dropped and turned a crooked smile his way. "Hey, lionman. I'm back. Did you miss me, kitty?"

Yes. Pleasure infused him at the sight of her, which was why he chose to focus instead on the stupid nicknames meant to provoke him.

It worked. He glared. "Go." The sound more bark than purr had the effect of making her laugh.

"No can do, lionman. You are my new assignment."

Meaning? What exactly was Jayda? He knew her as Cerberus's daughter only. Thus far, a wily female who shouldn't be underestimated.

A danger to him. "Go," he repeated, keeping it simple unlike the tumultuous thoughts running in his head.

She tilted her head, lips still partially upturned. "Go? But we haven't even got started. And I had such fun things planned." She winked.

In some ways he was still a man. Marcus thanked the fact a sheet pinned him tight. A man shouldn't get hard when a woman verbally tortured him.

He blamed the fact he'd been without for too

long. Why else would he be attracted to the one who'd brought him back to the lab? He should hate her for returning him to where his troubles began.

"Go away." He bit out the words, short and sharp, while knowing they wouldn't do a damned thing.

A part of him was glad she shook her head. "Don't be a pussy. You are stuck with me. Because, apparently, you're a bit of a snob and have been giving everyone else the silent treatment."

Dammit. Someone had observed him with Jayda and now thought to use her against him.

Fight her allure. He glared.

She smiled wider. "Poor kitty. Did we get off on the wrong foot? What do you say we start over? Hi. I'm Jayda Cerberus. My dad is your doctor."

"I know." She stood before him as a reminder he was weak when it came to revenge.

"This is where you tell me your name," she prodded.

"You know who I am."

"A whiny-ass bitch apparently." She rolled her eyes.

That stung. "I haven't complained."

"No, you haven't," she agreed. "You've just been letting yourself die, bit by bit. Why?" The bluntness of the question took him by surprise.

"Why not?"

"Because it makes no sense. Look at you." She waved in his direction. "You're a big, strong man in his prime. Seems like a reason to live to me."

"Not a man."

She smirked. "Why? Because your eyes glow in the dark? Because your hair is thick and lush?"

How to explain it was more than the physical. How he felt, how he saw things had changed.

"I'm different inside."

"Feeling as if there's something inside you trying to get out? A wild beast that, if allowed free rein, will steal who you are, never letting you back in the driver seat again?"

He glanced at her sharply. How had she explained it so well? Then again, no surprise. Look at her father. "How do you know?"

"You are not the first. Nor the last. Do you know how many other people have come through here? Been a recipient of the treatment?"

"Too many."

"According to who? You?" She arched a brow. "You and all the other patients were given the chance of a lifetime. The cure of all cures."

"It's only a cure if the side effects aren't worse."

"Seriously?" She ogled him. "You're going to tell

me that lying in a hospital bed in a permanent coma and vegetative state is better than what you are now? Come on, kitty, why don't you lie to my face and say you'd rather still be pissing in a bag, stuck in your own head?"

He struggled because she was right. In so many respects he was better off. He could move and talk and feel. While, at the same time, he was a prisoner with limited abilities to communicate who felt despair and loneliness.

"I'm still a prisoner, just with different bars holding me."

"It doesn't have to be like this." She placed a hand on the restraint over his chest. Not touching, and yet so close.

"I just need to be a good, obedient patient." He sighed. "Do you have any idea how hard it is to have someone controlling your freedom?"

"Only because you don't control yourself."

"Is that all it takes? In that case, scout's honor, I'll behave. Now untie me." He gave only a slight tug at the restraints. No point in taxing himself when he only wanted to prove a point.

She glanced at the cuffs then him. "Here's the thing. I already know what would happen. I let you go, and you'll do something stupid, like attack me, which wouldn't end well. For you. Or you'll attack someone else, which again, results in a bad end for you."

"And?" he asked.

"I think that would be a shame, Marcus Bouvier." Gripping the handrails, she hauled herself close. Close enough to his ear that, when she whispered, it tickled the lobe. "You have a lot to offer. And I have so much to give."

Cryptic words that followed her out.

Leaving him alone. Aware. Awake. He might never sleep again.

When the door hummed as someone new entered, he found himself eager to see Jayda again. Eager for something.

Only to be vastly disappointed as Dr. Chimera himself strode into view, hands tucked behind his back. Smug smile on his face.

"Marcus, delighted to see you're doing better," he declared.

Damn the doctors and their spying. The rage proved quick, and the beast within rose with a fiercely grumbled, "Grghdgdge." Which, in monster language, stood for "I hate you and want to suck the marrow out of your bones."

The suave Dr. Chimera didn't react and kept a cautious distance in spite of the restraints.

"What want?" He purposely stilted the

words. Confused by the ins and outs of his mental acuity. Why had he gone from monosyllables to full thoughts and sentences again? The reason—the person, he should say—made no sense.

"Given the sudden change in your status, I thought I'd come for a visit."

"Go."

"I can't leave yet, Marcus. We haven't discussed the new treatment you're about to try."

"No medicine."

"Oh, we're well past that point. I don't think I have a serum to fix your issues. You'll have to fix them on your own. I'd hoped your time in the woods would help clear your mind. That obviously didn't work out."

"Escape again." Perhaps that was the answer, to remove himself once more from the clinic and let nature take its course.

"Your optimism is noted and misplaced. I won't be letting you go again." Chimera arched a brow. "Haven't you realized yet that your escape was orchestrated?"

Marcus shook his head and bared his teeth as he snarled, "No." Because there was nothing easy about it. Desperate, he'd killed to get out of the clinic. He and the other monsters shed blood on their path to freedom. Even Chimera wasn't so cold as to condone that.

"I have to commend you on not taking the expected route out of the building. Shame those guards didn't stand down as ordered." Oddly enough, there was a hint of remorse in those words.

"You let me go?" The very idea seemed ludicrous.

"Why not? It occurred to me that you weren't thriving in captivity. Which made me wonder, perhaps the cage was the problem. But I couldn't just release you. You had to want to run away. To leave and live in the mountains. Or if you actually managed to make it out of the range, fit in with society or die. Instead, you came back." Chimera fixed him with a stare. "Why?"

A question he still struggled with. "Not an animal." Even if he'd burrowed like one for months in the wilderness. Struggling because he'd escaped as winter left the land. Growing fat all summer on the plenteousness of nature, only to dread the coming chill that would sleep the land.

"No, you're not an animal. You're still smart. I can see that mind of yours working in there. What I don't understand is why you play dumb."

"Not dumb," he spat.

"Really?" Chimera stood closer and stared at

him, not having to tilt too much being a tall man himself. "Not dumb, yet you returned to be caught. Not dumb, yet you didn't take the chance to escape."

"I got rid of the tracker." Pride lit his words. Bet that fucker didn't expect that.

"Indeed, you did. Seems we didn't hide them as well as we thought. Luke also rid himself of his. Here's to hoping he doesn't regret it." Chimera shook his head. "But he and the cub his woman carry aren't your concern. You're my priority right now. I want to know why it is when Jayda is in the room you become more coherent."

Marcus denied it. "Not."

"I've watched the video. Each time she's around, you become yourself again. More man, less beast."

Was it that noticeable? What did it mean?

"I wonder if it's something in the pheromones she exudes. Tell me, Marcus"—Adrian leaned forward, his expression conspiratorial—"do you want to fuck her?"

The suggestion painted an erotic image and caused an instant erection.

Ruined as Adrian said, "I wouldn't blame you. She has a smoking body."

A body he could picture oh so well.

"Rumor has it she's popular with the guards."

"Good for her." He wanted to clamp his lips tight as the words emerged more growly than expected.

"I'm surprised you think so." Adrian's tone turned sly. "I thought you were attracted to her."

"Nope." He lied. Lied hard.

"So you're not bothered at all by the thought of her getting naked for another man? Perhaps getting on her knees. Begging him—"

The roar erupted suddenly as the meat sack dared to go too far.

Adrian arched a brow but didn't flinch. "Well. That was interesting."

No, it wasn't. It meant nothing. She meant nothing.

But it was too late to say anything. Chimera left, leaving him alone. With his thoughts.

Fantasies.

Desires.

CHAPTER ELEVEN

"WELL. THAT WAS INTERESTING," SHE HEARD Adrian say for the third time. The video she kept replaying had sound, action, and just missed popcorn. As to why she kept replaying the meeting between Adrian and Marcus? Jayda found kitty's reactions interesting.

For one, he remained more or less coherent, speaking in full sentences and making sense.

She discovered he was smart. Not only had he managed to survive in the wild, he'd figured out the tracker the clinic fitted all its projects with. Staff, too.

Just one of those things the brochure didn't mention and that the contract didn't cover. It was administered during a round of vaccinations, the tiny chip floating around the body. Only one technician got unlucky enough to have it lodge in the brain.

Marcus, the lionman who escaped to the woods, apparently knew he had to disable it. And how. Made her wonder what he'd done exactly.

Re-watching him, Jayda remembered his reactions with her. His words and emotions clearly portrayed his resentment. Marcus suffered from a bitterness steeped in his belief that he could never have a normal life.

He was right, to a certain extent. So long as he behaved like an animal, he'd be treated like one, kept confined and out of harm's way.

That was only one possibility. Should he achieve control, the possibilities opened up. Jayda wasn't the only person with genetic modifications who travelled the world, as free as a person could be. Look at Adrian, the very first project of all, still running the clinic with an iron fist and steely resolve.

A person with the will could learn. She could teach him. Show him how to harness the beast instead of existing as a dichotomy, opposing sides constantly in battle.

The only problem with that plan was Marcus himself. He claimed he didn't want anything. He asked for freedom and yet didn't really push the issue.

The only time he truly perked up was when she

engaged him. And the only time he truly got upset was when Adrian talked dirty about her.

Jealousy. An interest in Jayda that she might be able to exploit.

She rewound and watched for a fourth time. Her father paused by her side, silently taking it in before frowning and saying, "That was disturbing. I'll have to speak to Adrian. His lack of respect for my daughter won't be tolerated."

"Please, we both know he was only baiting Marcus."

"That doesn't make it right."

"It did teach us something interesting. Marcus showed jealousy."

"Over you?" Her father laughed. "I highly doubt the prisoner desires his jailor, no matter what Adrian says."

"He responds to me." Something that still had the ability to warm her inside.

"He also responded to Adrian."

True. "You were right. He's still redeemable."

"I wouldn't be so sure of that. Did you see how his face changed when he got upset?" Her father leaned in and played with the mouse, rewinding the video to the moment when Marcus roared, his eyes blazing with green fire, his mouth open wide over pronounced incisors. His nose flattened, and his hair poofed into a golden halo. A veritable mane.

"And? We both know intense emotions bring out physical characteristics, but that isn't an indication of mental acuity."

"His blood test shows the DNA strand took too well to the grafts. He's truly more animal than man."

"So am I, and you let me off the leash."

"Sometimes I wonder if that was a mistake," he muttered.

"Love you too, Daddy," she mocked.

"When do you leave?" he asked, changing the subject.

"Trying to get rid of me?" She leaned back in the chair and arched a brow. "But I was just getting started with Marcus."

"That ends now. After what Adrian said..." Her father shook his head. "Him putting dirty ideas like that in Marcus's head. That was wrong."

"I don't think you can exactly be stating what's right or wrong." Loving him dearly didn't make her blind to his faults.

"Family should be off-limits."

"Since when?" He'd never hesitated in the past to use family to advance his goals. It didn't work so well with Mommy.

He shot her a look. "That was different." He'd

used Jayda as a test subject to save her life. It didn't make it more legal. But it had kept her alive.

However, curing her didn't make her more likely to just swallow his bullshit.

"Different only because you say so. Problem is, I'm not a kid anymore, Daddy. You don't get to tell me what to do. Wasn't it you that said sometimes the rules must be bent if science is to advance?"

"Offering you up as some kind of tasty bait isn't advancement."

She propped her booted feet onto the desk and leaned farther back. "You didn't have a problem with it when you called me in and asked me to dangle myself in front of him to get him out of the woods."

"Because it should have been a controlled situation. You were to draw him out and tranq him. Instead, you let him catch you off guard and allowed yourself to be kidnapped."

So he'd noticed she'd let the lionman take her. "I was curious to see what he'd do. You and Adrian seemed at odds over whether or not he can be saved. He's not a savage killer." The guard who'd gone missing during his capture was found, sporting a goose egg and dehydrated, but alive.

"The fact he didn't immediately begin gnawing on your limbs doesn't mean he wouldn't have killed you."

"Would you have missed me, Daddy?" She batted her lashes. She was sure in his own way, her father cared about her. It just wasn't the warm and huggy kind of love that other families shared.

He pressed his lips into a flat line. "You are impossible to talk to. While you might not believe me, I don't want you to get hurt. I'm not a monster."

"Are you sure? Because you are the maker of them." Daddy had also been partaking of some of the special juice. The signs of his age reversing were too much to ignore.

"I create miracles." The lie that helped him sleep at night.

Jayda rolled her eyes. "Save that line for your money-bag donors. You're a Dr. Moreau. And Marcus is your lionman. Emphasis on man. I think we can save him still." Why she even wanted to was not something she understood. Why did she keep fighting? Was this just her stubbornness in the face of her father's refusal? Or was something more at play?

"Moments of lucidity don't mean Marcus can recover. He wavers in and out of acuity."

"Which we need to work on. He seems to do better when directly engaged I've noticed."

"With you and Adrian. Everyone else gets the silent treatment." Said with clear disgruntlement.

Daddy let Marcus get under his skin. Usually that was her specialty.

"Which again is a conscious choice on his part. Showing command. I think we can expand that control."

"How? What's your plan? Go in each day to talk with him?" Heavy on the sarcasm.

"I don't have a plan. I was going to wing it." She wasn't a doctor or therapist, just a person who'd dealt with her own monster.

"Ten years of medical school, double that in the lab, and you think you can accomplish with Marcus what I haven't?" he sneered. "Go right ahead."

She would. Because she had to. Having seen Marcus again, she couldn't stop thinking about him. Wondering at her strange fascination. Her desire.

An arousal satisfied in the shower that did nothing to sate her hunger. Only one person could do that.

She waited until the next day, late morning, before striding into his room. But she didn't raise his bed.

"Hey, kitty, how did you sleep?" she asked, noting the craggy lines of his face. The change in him physically was remarkable. She'd seen the before photos. A scrawny man, myopic, his skin pitted with scars.

Now a tawny hunk, his golden mane spread over the pillow.

She tugged a golden lock, and despite his eyes being shut, faking sleep, he growled, low and sexy. The kind of growl that vibrated a girl's parts.

Naughty kitty. She patted him on the cheek. "Be a good boy and maybe we can get around to taking off those restraints.

"Grawr." He made another noise, meant to be animal like, yet it lacked the true guttural timber of the wild.

"Are you really going to play games with me, kitty?" She vaulted onto the bed and sat on him, legs splayed, her core pressed right on his groin—where an erection said hello.

Probably making Daddy gnash his teeth if he watched, but it served its purpose as it got Marcus's attention.

"Get off."

"Are you offering or asking?" she sassed, leaning forward so that her hair fell in a curtain and framed them.

"Go away."

"Can't do that, kitty. I told you, you're my assignment. Getting paid a pretty penny, too. You're awfully important to some people."

"Using me," he sneered.

"Which is the way of the world. I mean look at how you're using me." Everyone had a tendency of using her. Mother as a pawn in the divorce. Adrian and her dad as a test subject. Now Marcus, as his reason for sanity.

He blinked. The man had incredibly thick lashes but only seen up close because of the blond.

"Oh, come on. Don't play innocent now. I've seen how you pretend to be some animal when I'm not around. Growling and snarling. And then, when I appear, magically coherent."

"Not you," he said, turning his head to the side.

But he couldn't escape her. She still pinned him and lowered her face close enough to almost brush his skin.

"If it's not me, then why is it all the sensors go haywire when I walk in the room? Your heart rate goes up. Your temperature spikes, and this"—she ground her hips against his groin, the erection clear—"is not something in your pocket."

"You mean nothing to me." The words spoken hotly and yet she smiled at the obvious lie in them.

"You should learn to lie better, kitty."

"Not a lie. I hate you. I'd kill you if given a chance."

"Then why haven't you?" She was close enough he could head butt, even tear at her with his teeth.

Instead, his reply emerged as a soft purr and that erection didn't suddenly disappear.

"I might be a monster, but I don't intentionally kill."

Funny, because she had the opposite mentality.

I am a monster who likes to kill. What she didn't like was rejection.

"If you could have one thing right now, what would it be? Pizza? Beer? Sex?" She ground her hips.

"Peace."

"And what would give you peace?" she asked. "Don't tell me going back to the way things were before. I read your file. You were a dweeb."

"That's an asshole thing to say."

She laughed. "But true. Barely above minimum wage job, hardly any friends, you spent most of your time online."

"Because it was fun. I enjoyed it."

"But what about human interaction? A relationship? Can't snuggle a game controller."

"You saw what I looked like. Not too many women interested in a short geek. And I was fine with that."

"Liar," she breathed hotly against him. "I think you lived that way because it was safe. You could hide and avoid the cruel world who saw you only for the shell housing your mind. But you're not that person anymore, kitty."

"You're right. I'm not. I'm not me. Or free. Or anything now."

"Which is the wrong attitude to take. You've been given a second chance. An opportunity to be someone new. To experience real life."

"Not interested."

"Are you sure about that?" She ground one last time against him.

"Leave me alone," snarled with frustration.

Kitty seemed to think he could lie and pretend. Daddy thought he could tell her what to do.

They'd learn.

CHAPTER TWELVE

"Later, kitty," she breathed on him, the words hot with promise, the heat of her igniting his skin. Enflaming his cock. He sucked in a breath as she ground herself against his groin.

And then nothing...she left.

Left him aching.

Awake.

Frustrated.

"Argggggh!" The roar emerged as a meld of emotions. The beast couldn't handle it. The man didn't understand either.

He shook in his manacles. Screamed at the ceiling. Wrung himself right out fighting against his prison and fate and the world.

It lasted hours. Hours where he roared at the nurses. Snapped at the guards. Made himself a virtual nuisance until suddenly he ran out of energy. He calmed enough to fall into a restless sleep, interrupted by the opening of his door.

Husky laughter softly rumbled from out of sight. The timbre of it immediately woke his dick.

Jayda had returned, and Marcus tensed. He watched for movement, not wanting her to catch him unaware. The lights in the room had dimmed, meaning it was night. Shadows hugged the corners and edges.

Listening hard, he caught the scuff of feet, another soft chuckle followed by the murmur of a man. "Are you sure we should be in here?"

What. The. Fuck. Jayda came here with another man!

He seethed. He just didn't understand why. As if he cared Jayda chose to be with a guy. He was pissed they'd disturbed his sleep.

Yup. That was why he simmered.

"He's probably passed out. And if he isn't, let him listen. I'm sure he'd enjoy the entertainment," Jayda sassed, and in that moment, he knew she did on purpose.

It didn't help the rising rage.

"Why not go back to your room instead?" the dead man suggested.

Yeah, he sounded pretty hale and hearty now.

But Marcus didn't see that lasting once he got out of these restraints.

"Don't tell me you're afraid," Jayda teased.

Be afraid, be very afraid. Marcus seethed, feeling the monster inside rising, and not tempted in the least to stop it.

"What about the cameras?" asked the hesitant fellow.

Just another reason to hate the fucker. He was a whiny little shit. She was practically handing herself to him on a silver fucking platter and the asshole was worried about getting caught.

"I put the electronic eyes for this level on a loop, so no one would see. Jesus, Wade, are you coming, or am I going to play with myself?" Said with a naughty lilt, promising delights...

...to another man.

Fabric tightened around his biceps, pulled at his thighs as his anger swelled. A few seams loosened across the breadth of his shoulders. The bands around his frame dug into his flesh.

"I'll follow you anywhere, baby."

"Don't call me, baby." Softly muttered, and yet he heard it as Jayda strode into view keeping her gaze ahead, not once looking at Marcus. He, on the other hand, drank her in.

She looked especially delicious tonight, the blue

jeans molding her lower body as if painted on. Her tank top just as snug. Her breasts high, her waist indented. She sported pink gloss on her lips.

She also wore a hand on her waist.

A guy's hand.

Touching her.

Marcus hissed, and all the hair on his body—an impressive amount—stood at attention.

Something began to creak, which caused Wade— the soon-to-be dead man—to look his way.

"Shit. He's awake."

Jayda cupped Wade's cheek and turned his face before he could see Marcus smile in welcome.

"Ignore him. He's just a big ol' pussy." Insulting Marcus and yet she still wouldn't look at him. Rather, she dragged the guard a little closer. Hopped her ass onto a counter and then planted Wade's hands on her hips so that he could snuggle in between her thighs. Fully clothed and yet the sexual suggestion was plain.

It made Marcus seethe that they would so openly tryst in front of him. He made a noise that kept the guy from leaning in for a kiss.

Wade shot Marcus a glance over his shoulder. "He's a big fucker."

"I wouldn't know. Never got to see his junk since he turned me down," Jayda remarked, her gaze finally meeting Marcus's, daring him, her lips upturned in challenge.

"Hold on." The guard turned back. "You telling me you would have banged one of the monsters?"

"You think he's a monster?" Jayda asked, hopping off the counter and moving to stand in front of Marcus. "That would imply he's fearsome. But look at him." She leaned close and activated the bed, tilting him. "Nothing but a man juiced on animal steroids. Barely coherent."

As if to add credence to her words, a rumbling sound emerged from Marcus.

"He's a beast, ain't he." The guard moved to stand in front of him. Obviously one of the newer fellows. Lanky. Handsome. Small compared to him. A crunchy meat sack.

Marcus bared his teeth, knowing the incisors were more pronounced. He had felt them biting the inside of his mouth.

"A lonely beast who hasn't been laid in forever." Jayda held Marcus's stare, her eyes a swirling pit of green and brown. Flat and emotionless. Waiting for him to react.

Everything got a little tighter: clothes, metal bands holding him. Something pinged. The guard missed seeing the wiggle as the band around Marcus's chest pulled loose.

"Let's give him something to watch," Wade remarked, reaching for Jayda.

She spun away and laughed. "How about first a show for both of you?" She shoved the guard so that he leaned against the counter. Jayda put her hands on the hem of her shirt.

What is she doing? Marcus could only stare, riveted, as she peeled fabric off, revealing breasts cupped high in a crimson bra. Her body lean and athletic. The muscles defined and smooth. Lickably smooth.

She tossed the shirt to the side and put her hands on her hips, showcasing her hourglass shape. The high round ass. "You think he likes what he sees?" The query asked of the guard, and yet she tossed Marcus a look over her bared shoulder, a challenge in her gaze.

"I know I'm liking." The guard began to unbutton his shirt, revealing a toned body but no bulk.

The bands dug into Marcus's skin a little deeper, and the manacle on his left wrist got super tight then popped.

Jayda didn't look at Marcus when she asked Wade, "Does it make you hot to see me playing with him?"

Yes. Yes, it does. Marcus ached. Wanted to sink

into her from behind, holding on to her hair and driving her hard until she arched and screamed.

"I'd be hotter if you touched me." Wade tossed his shirt to the floor.

A low sound rumbled out of him, and Jayda whirled. "Hear that? The lion is awake. And hungry." Hips swaying, Jayda drew close to Marcus, close enough to tease a nail down a section of his chest, scraping over taut fabric that parted as if sliced away by her touch.

The pad of her finger then dragged backwards over his exposed flesh, drawing a shiver that made the whole bed tremble.

"Are you sure you should be touching him?" Hesitant Wade returned.

But Jayda wasn't a coward like Wade. She still touched. And she stared.

They both did, an intense gaze that locked them together.

"Can you imagine what it's like only being able to watch?" she mused aloud. "For him to see a woman touching and being touched. To know he'll never ever get to feel that pleasure."

"Fucking torture," Wade agreed.

"Actually, that's teasing. This would be torture." She whirled to face Wade once more, putting her back to Marcus.

But she didn't walk away. Rather she bent down, one hand touching the floor, the perfection of her rounded butt in the air. Jayda had no intention of stopping there.

That ass, perched perfectly atop her long legs, made longer in the heeled boots she wore, was just the right height.

It cupped into his groin perfectly. Ground into him, forcing Marcus to draw in a sharp breath. Then no breath at all as she wiggled and waggled.

"That's it, baby," Wade crowed. "Twerk him. Fuck, that's cruel."

It was cruel. Not only could Marcus *not* sink into that evident invitation but he couldn't kill Wade yet.

He couldn't do a damned thing, not while she still gyrated against him. She glanced over her shoulder, catching his eye, winking, grinding.

Teasing.

The pre-orgasm shudder shook the bed again.

Imagine how it would be if he actually got to touch her.

"You are so fucking hot." Wade, the cock blocker, shoved off the counter toward Jayda, his expression smoldering with desire.

The fucker is starting to piss me off. What Marcus was thinking, yet what emerged from his mouth was, "Grawr."

Standing, Jayda let Wade get close enough to put his hands on her bare skin.

My skin.

The cracking and popping of the rest of his restraints wasn't as loud as the thud of his feet when he hit the ground.

The peek Jayda gave over her shoulder didn't look surprised at all, but the meat sack? His mouth dropped, and he made some kind of startled noise. "Shit—"

That was more than enough. Marcus shot out a hand and grabbed the male who sniffed around his female. Dangled him off the floor by the throat. The squeezing stopped the sounds coming from it. The fingers clawing at him didn't disturb in the least.

"*Kitty.*" A word with stern overtones. "Be good." The female of the delicious scent made noises that he understood and ignored.

The meat sack in his fist kicked. So it got shaken into compliance.

The female placed a hand on his arm, the smooth touch drawing his attention. He looked down at her.

"That's a good, kitty. Look at Jayda," she crooned. "Let the man go."

His brow furrowed, and he shot a glance at the meat sack whose eyes bulged.

"Let him go, Marcus." The firm tone brought a low growl.

But it was the tweak of a nipple—that didn't stop but kept on being twisted—that brought a yelp.

He glanced down to see she held him firmly. He could yank free easily enough. After all, he was the bigger, stronger of them.

But that might injure the female.

"I said let go!" The twisting got more intense.

With a rumbling mini roar, he dropped the meat sack, who heaved on the floor, sucking in ragged breaths.

"Good boy." The pain in his nipple didn't disappear when she let go. The throb had him glaring at the female.

"Grawr."

"Don't be a pussy."

The female mocked his pain. He reached for her breast, only to have his hand slapped away.

"Doesn't work two ways, big guy. Now, can you talk?"

He pressed his lips tight.

"But you understand me?"

Did he?

"Don't pretend now. I'll bet if I said you could grab a boob you'd understand pretty fucking quick."

His gaze dropped to her chest.

Her soft chuckle meant she saw. "Still a man, I see. And just so we're clear, that wasn't permission."

He glanced at Wade scrambling across the floor. About time he left.

Her hand cupped Marcus's cheek, drawing his attention. "How much of you is in there right now?" she mused aloud.

Enough to know this woman had something special about her. He raised a hand to brush knuckles down her loose hair. The texture of it pleased. He curled a chunk of it around his finger, winding tighter and tighter.

Her turn to draw in a sharp note of pain as he reeled her close.

But she didn't protest. She stared at him, eyes wide and lips parted.

"How much of this will you remember?" She ran her hand over his cheek. "Amazing. I've never seen someone take on so many characteristics before. Even more lion now than in the cave."

She kept talking. Her lips moving, and all he wanted to do was capture those words.

He dipped his head, got close to her mouth, his gaze locked with hers.

Before he could press his lips to hers, an alarm sounded. *Whoop. Whoop.* His chin angled sharply as he tested the air.

Jayda cursed and pulled free from him. "Mother-humping little whore. Fucking Wade pulled an alarm."

"Should kill." The words guttural. The meaning clear.

She cast him a smirk. "Apparently. Next time I'll listen to you, but this time, you need to get behind me."

"Behind?" One incredulous word, given he loomed much larger than her. His earlier rage had triggered the shift that changed his body. Meaning he'd gained a few inches all over.

"I know I'm not the ideal-sized shield, kitty, but they probably won't shoot you if I'm in the way. At least they better not."

Shoot?

The very suggestion someone would aim a weapon at Jayda bristled inside Marcus, drew the monster back to a pulsing head. Which was why, when the guards appeared with their guns drawn, yelling, "Don't move," he tossed her behind him and then jumped toward them with a roar.

CHAPTER THIRTEEN

Jayda should have known Marcus would try and be a hero.

Monster my ass, she thought as he strove to stand between her and the tranquilizers being shot by the guards.

And look at that, someone brought a Taser to the fight, too.

It wasn't helping. Marcus had enough adrenaline to handle the sleeping darts and the voltage.

Someone was going to get hurt.

Jayda strode toward the melee and punched the guy with the Taser first. His high-pitched cry drew attention, as did the blood spurting from his nose. Wade appeared behind the kneeling pussy and exclaimed, "I got help."

"You fucking moron," she seethed. "What the fuck did you do?"

"I saved you," Wade said.

Wrong answer. "I can save myself," Jayda hissed. She hauled back an arm to punch him, only to curse as Marcus flung himself at Wade.

They hit the floor in a tussle that wouldn't last long. *Rap. Rap.* Wade's eyes rolled back. Someone took offense and yelled, "Fucking monster!"

Marcus shot off for his next target.

This was getting ridiculous. Jayda shoved two fingers in her mouth and whistled.

Everyone stilled. Even Marcus froze, his fist pulled back, ready to punch.

With all eyes on her, she snapped, "Everybody get the fuck out before I volunteer your asses for the next round of experiments. I hear they're thinking of splicing with cockroaches."

Bodies scattered, as people obviously came to their limited senses and realized she wasn't to be messed with.

Marcus didn't leave. Rather he stalked toward Wade, who'd risen to his feet and pointed. "You can't leave him loose. He's an animal."

An animal provoked, which meant she didn't blame him for his actions. On the other hand, she wasn't too happy with Wade, which was why she let

Marcus slap his head off the wall a few times before saying, "Let him go."

"Don't like him," Marcus said, the guttural words hard to understand.

"Me either."

"Hey!" Wade protested through bloody lips.

Marcus grinned, his teeth rather pronounced. Definitely a carnivore and yet he'd not eaten anyone. There might be hope for him yet.

"Let the little man go."

Marcus released Wade, who stumbled before righting himself. "I'm going to tell—"

She interrupted. "You complain, and you'll disappear without a trace. Your contract states implicitly that you are to follow orders. And right now, that includes my orders. So listen carefully, little man, do your job and do it well, or I'm going to bring you back to visit Marcus and next time I won't intervene."

"Bitch," Wade breathed, only to scurry from the room as Marcus leaned close with a growl.

With Wade gone, they were alone, and Jayda sighed as she noted how many darts stuck out of the lionman's body. Once he calmed down, the drugs would kick in. "Kitty, you are going to have to learn to control that temper of yours."

"Not angry," he slurred, taking a step toward her and then wavering in place. "Protecting."

"I'm not the one that needs protecting," she noted, darting quickly to support him. The tatters of his scrubs dangled from his body.

She half carried him over to the bed and then helped him fall on it.

"No wanna sleep." His eyes fought to stay open.

"Then you should have listened to me. Take a nap, and we'll have a chat when you wake up."

"Stay." He reached for her, and she grasped his hand. Stared down at the strange and intimate interlacing of their fingers.

"I'm not leaving." Not yet. But staring down at the sleeping Marcus, she had to wonder at her urge to stay.

Especially when her father laid into her the next morning.

"What were you thinking?" her daddy snapped, pacing in front of her, replaying the camera feed. She'd lied to Wade when she said she'd stopped it. How else could she study the subject later and truly get a feel for his reactions?

And holy shit did she get lots to study. Her plan to engage Marcus's baser instincts worked all too well. She watched and rewatched as her every move seemed to incite Marcus until he snapped.

Yet not once did he do anything untoward to Jayda. On the contrary, his first instinct was... "To protect me," she mused aloud, watching again as Marcus jumped between her and the guards.

While she found the videos fascinating and useful, her father glanced at them and then harangued. "What did I say about getting intimately involved with Marcus?"

"How do you figure I'm involved?" she asked. "I brought Wade down there to have sex. Not my fault you didn't have Marcus tied down well enough."

In that moment, her father, and not the doctor, eyed Jayda, expression a flat mask. "We both know you did it on purpose. Marcus is attracted to you. You intentionally set him off."

"Yes, but did you see how much better he behaved than in the past?" Much better. No one died.

"What I saw was you getting lucky."

Not really. If she'd gotten lucky, she wouldn't have needed her showerhead the night before.

She turned off the video and stood to confront her father. "Adrian told me to deal with Marcus. So I am."

"Provoking him so that the beast comes out isn't what I call helping him," her father retorted hotly.

"Keeping him calm won't prepare him. He needs to learn control."

"Let him learn from someone else."

"What's this? Are you showing paternal concern?" Jayda mocked. "Funny how selective you are about when it applies. When you wanted to catch Marcus, you were all for my doing anything I could to give a hand. Now that I'm to work intimately with him in your place, you're having a jealousy fit."

"It's not jealousy. The man is dangerous."

Very. It was one of his most redeeming traits.

"I'm also dangerous. Which is why Adrian has trusted me with this. Pity you don't have faith enough in me, too."

"This has nothing to do with my belief in your abilities. I think you being around him is dangerous for your own recovery."

Her tone went flat. "There is nothing wrong with me."

"You're different."

"No duh," she mocked.

Her father bristled. "You know it's more than the treatment. I really wish you'd talk to Dr. Griffon."

"A head shrink?" Her lip curled. "There nothing wrong with my mind."

"What about your emotions?" he asked. "The fact you lack empathy—"

"Makes me excellent at my job. And what makes you think I had much before?"

Pre-treatment, Jayda lacked the courage of conviction when it came to follow through. After her treatment, it became easy to accomplish anything she put her mind to. Even if it involved killing.

"I worry about you." A softly made admission that brought her close enough to put her hand on his arm.

"And I worry about you, Daddy." She looked him in the eye and broached the reality of what he'd done. "Have you heard the other voice yet?" The one she'd immediately embraced because of its strength. But others, like Marcus, had fought it.

"I am perfectly sane. And so are you." As if by mere force of will he could make it so. Perhaps he could. When she'd been a young girl, her daddy always did seem invincible. Look at him, curing her when all the doctors claimed she would die.

Her hero.

And pain in the ass.

"If you don't think I'm crazy, then why not give me some room to work with? You need my help," Jayda insisted.

Her father sighed, looking old despite his more youthful features. "Be careful."

"Never." Her favorite answer. "So how's he doing this morning?"

"He's not yet woken from the darts."

"But he's okay?" she asked, needing confirmation.

Her father nodded. "While he was sleeping, we had a new room prepared for him. A more secure one."

"With thicker chains?" She shook her head. "No thanks. I want him out of level six."

The laughter proved sharp. Her father still chuckled as he said, "No way."

"I don't know how you expect me to make progress when he's tied down like a criminal on his way to an execution."

"Better he be tied than free to go on a rampage and kill everyone he finds."

"Ah, look at you, pretending to have a conscience." She patted her father's cheek. "It's cute. You are also assuming I'll fail. I won't. However, to get Marcus to trust me, I need to give him something. A gift to show what is possible."

"You are not taking him out of level six. If you want him out of the chains, then we'll put him in the bunker." The nickname for the room made entirely of concrete. Bed, table, stools. The only thing a patient could throw was a tantrum with his pillow.

Given she'd aimed high, hoping for this exact outcome, she controlled her features as she sighed and said, "The bunker works, but I want to be the only one allowed inside."

That compressed her father's lips. "He still needs to be studied."

"You'll have to do it from afar. Like I said, I need him to trust me if I want him to listen. Besides, you don't need daily blood from him."

"We also don't need sperm samples." Her father's crude words wrinkled her nose.

"Ew, Daddy. Really."

"I meant it, Jayda. No sex with him. Especially him. There's no telling what might happen if the two of you..." He trailed off, so she finished.

"Had sex." She raised her gaze heavenward. "God forbid I find a guy who can handle me and might give me an orgasm."

That brought a ruddy hue to her dad's cheeks. "Jayda!"

"What? Don't play innocent. You know what happened to that guy I dated." The first one she had sex with after she recovered from the treatments. Poor Perry still had to breathe through a tube.

"You just need to curb your strength."

But that was the problem. She didn't want to hold back.

"Don't worry, Daddy. Now when I break someone, I make sure they never find the body."

That brought a heavy sigh. "I swear you do it on purpose."

Sometimes she did.

"There is another way to get him to trust you," her father offered. "We could always try a dream walk. We've had it recently work with success."

Let someone mess with her head? No thanks. Besides, why have dream fun with Marcus when she could have the real thing?

"I don't trust that chick and her dream thing." Another Chimera secret. "I'll stick to the old-fashioned methods."

"Hmmph." Her father made a sound that said everything he felt. Including the one that made her hug him from behind.

"Love you, too, Daddy." Releasing him, she strode to the door. "I'm going to check on Marcus."

"Try and keep your clothes on this time."

"Ah, Daddy. Why you trying to ruin all my fun?"

CHAPTER FOURTEEN

Marcus woke to Jayda crouching atop him, lightly slapping his cheek. "Rise and shine, kitty."

"Go away. I was having a nice nap." He twisted onto his side, only moderately surprised when it worked. Apparently his subconscious noticed the lack of fetters. Jayda managed to roll with his body and ended up on her side beside him on the foam mattress barely wide enough for two.

Worried she might fall, he placed a hand on her waist.

Why did he care?

He shoved her off.

She didn't completely fall. Jayda rose, put her elbows on the mattress, and grinned at him. "Feeling better?"

Not really. Having her near just reminded him

of how fucking hard she made him. How much he wanted her. The fact that his hands were free with a bed under him.

He glanced at the camera sitting over the door, the red light a reminder they weren't actually alone.

Perhaps her daddy watched.

The very idea had him reaching out to tug her close, murmuring, "I know what would make me feel better."

Her laughter wasn't a blow job or even a kiss. But he enjoyed it nonetheless. "You are a bad kitty. I see what you're doing. Thinking you can piss off my daddy by diddling with his daughter."

"Two birds. One stone." He gave her a crooked smile. "Got any issues you'd like to act out?"

"Many, but not today. Today is about dealing with your jealousy."

That got him to stiffen and roll away from her. "I don't suffer from jealousy because I don't give a shit about anything. Or anyone."

"So last night you weren't bothered at all by the fact I was going to bang some other guy? Let him put his hands all over me?"

Marcus never even realized he moved. He hauled her close, his lips brushing hers as he growled. "Don't."

"Don't what, kitty?" she teased.

"Push me over the edge. You might not like what you see."

"I might surprise you," she murmured in reply

"Why do you keep coming back?" He really didn't understand. For all that his mind had cleared, and he could think again, he couldn't decipher what game she played.

"Told you, you're my current assignment."

"You're not a doctor."

"Nope." She popped the p. "Not even close. But I do have experience in dealing with demons."

The word did more to recoil him than anything. "So now I'm evil?"

"Stop being so bloody melodramatic." She stalked around the bed to face him. "I was talking about the demons up here." She tapped her temple.

"What would you know about them?" he sneered. "What would you know about any of this?" He swept a hand.

"Have you forgotten who my dad is?"

"As if I could ever forget his face. He's the one who did this to me."

"Then we have something in common. My dad experimented on me, too."

At the claim, he laughed. "Nice try, *baby*." He used the word intentionally, and her expression stiffened.

"Don't call me that," Jayda spat, her body bristling.

"Tell you what, I'll stop when you use my name instead of kitty."

"But kitty is a nice name. Means I think you're soft and cuddly."

"Don't forget I have sharp claws."

"You going to carve me up?" she asked, baring her throat.

A nice throat. A long, mocha strip with a pulse beating in the base of it.

"Go away."

"Why would I do that when we're having such a fascinating conversation?"

Him conversing, and with someone who didn't need him to hide what he was. What a concept.

"You can't fix me. This isn't a mental issue."

"Nope, because there's nothing wrong with your mind. It's your impulse control that needs work." She flopped on the bed, making herself comfortable in direct opposite to him.

"I can control myself just fine." Despite how delicious she appeared lying there, he didn't pounce on her.

"Says the guy who jumped in front of a bunch of guards armed with guns."

"Don't worry. Had it been bullets, I would have used you as a shield." Such a lie.

Jayda caught it. "Oh, kitty, you are such a bad liar. Something else I'll have to teach you."

"Why are you really here?" he asked. "What do you get out of this?"

"A paycheck."

"So you'll compromise your morals for money?"

"Doesn't everyone?" The guileless wide-eyed stare almost brought a chuckle.

"What makes you qualified to help?" A horrid idea hit him, and he gaped at her. "You're a shrink."

"Most definitely not. Your horrified tone matches my thoughts about them."

"So why you?"

"Because you wouldn't talk to anyone else for starters. And because you apparently missed me saying it the first time. I'm special like you."

"No, you're not." Too quickly he realized how it sounded. To his surprise, she didn't appear offended.

She laughed. "Oh, how wrong you are. What do you see when you look at me?"

Perfection.

But instead he said, "A cocky lady who thinks it's a wise idea to be in a room with me."

"You won't hurt me."

"You don't know that for sure," he argued. It

bothered she didn't take him seriously as a threat. At the same time, it pleased she didn't fear him.

"You need to stop seeing yourself as some kind of murdering monster. Unless you enjoy it?" She pierced him with a stare. "Do you like killing things, kitty? Tearing them apart and licking your claws after?"

He gaped at her. "No." Which was only partially true. The human side of him hated the violence. But the feline half...

"I enjoy controlled chaos," she admitted.

"Meaning?"

She shrugged. "Meaning, when I kill, I do it because it's expedient and necessary. Not out of emotion."

He snickered. "Trying to convince me you're a serial killer with no remorse? As if."

"Why not?"

For many reasons, he stuck to facts. "Historically, women are unlikely to be the perpetrators of mass murder."

"Unlikely, but it happens. And it's not murder. Murder implies an emotional act. I kill for other reasons. Like money. Or to preserve a secret."

Arguing seemed futile. He'd seen her act the night before. How she not only acquitted herself barehanded but had dominated the situation.

She must have gotten the good version of the serum. Beautiful and assertive. What she failed to realize, but he noticed, was she didn't turn into a monster to fight.

He did.

"I'm not sure what a company killer is supposed to teach me. Or is this about recruitment? Does Chimera need more assassins?"

"Probably."

"I won't become his pet killer. So you might as well give up now."

"If you're going to be this difficult, then maybe I should blow this joint and go back to my real life."

"Must be nice to have that option," he muttered.

She rolled onto her stomach and watched him as he paced his new room. "Your life doesn't have to be like this."

"Is this where you tell the monster if he's a good boy he'll get to play outside?" The sarcasm rolled thickly off his tongue.

"It's happened with others. Behave and you get freedom."

"Freedom to do what?" he snorted. "I've been missing, probably presumed dead, for how long now? I have nowhere to go." All his video games, his comfy chair, everything he used to own probably donated or trashed.

"Cry me a river. Having roots is overrated."

"Says the woman with a father. And I'll wager you have friends."

"My dad and I have a strange relationship. As to friend,"—she shrugged—"you'd only be partially right. I have acquaintances. I'm not a person who gets along with too many folks. Kind of like you. I read your file. No real family to speak of. Dad took off when you were young. Your mom got remarried when you were a teen. Came to visit you once in the hospital, and that was to sign you over to the Chimaeram Clinic. Your friends were mostly the online variety."

His lips stiffened into flat lines. "Calling me a loser?"

"Just saying you and I are more alike than you think."

"Not even close. You get to walk out that door any time you want."

"What if you could, too?"

There was the dangling carrot. He didn't grab it. "We both know that won't happen."

"Not with that attitude it won't."

"Not ever. Those running the joint won't want me spilling any secrets."

"True." She didn't deny it. "That's the price to pay for our second life. But there's another reason to keep your mouth shut. Do you know what the real world does to people who claim they're monsters?"

He'd seen enough movies and played enough video games to answer this one. "Yeah, I know. Padded cell and pudding with no spoon. Except I can actually show them I'm not crazy."

She laughed. "I wasn't talking about a mental institute. There's more than one kind of cell. And if you think Chimaeram is mean, you should see what the government likes to do." She whistled. "They make my dad look like a Good Samaritan."

The point she made reminded him of the science fiction movies he loved to watch. The reality of what his world could be if he ever did speak. "Thanks for pointing out my life is fucked."

"Only if you're a rat. So don't be a rat."

He rolled his eyes. "Tell that to Chimera and your dad. Who knows what they've injected me with."

The poor jest made her smile. "They must have used something whiny because you have a serious case of the woe-is-me. You should be happy they intervened. You almost became body parts for the highest bidder."

"Meaning?"

"If we hadn't come along, your mother was planning to sell off your organs. Adrian happened to catch her just in time and made a better offer."

It shouldn't have surprised him to hear, and yet it still hurt. "I don't believe you." Surely his mother wouldn't do that to him? Wouldn't someone have told him?

"Don't believe. I don't care. You have the right to shove your head up your ass. I've heard the tapes. I read your file. I know all about you, kitty."

"Then you know I was a loser." His high school picture with his Coke-bottle glasses and shit haircut said it all. He didn't go much further than grade twelve, dropping out of college. Marcus was a nobody, working a nothing job, with no girlfriend, no life when the accident happened.

"You were uninspired," Jayda corrected. "You hadn't achieved your full potential."

At the claim, he chuckled. "You're right. I hadn't turned into a blood-thirsty monster."

"You forgot the cute part."

He blinked. "Excuse me?"

"Sorry would you prefer banging? Handsome?" She arched her brow in between asking. "Take a look in a mirror. You're a hottie now."

The claim took him by surprise, mostly because no woman had ever said those words to him.

Ever.

Not even close.

Which was why he didn't believe it now. "You're saying that to butter me up."

"If I wanted to butter you up, kitty, I'd be stroking you until you purred."

He asked, just because he must have misunderstood. "You think I'm attractive?"

"Physically, but don't worry, mentally, you're still a dork. Play your cards right and you'll be back to playing games online in no time. Hitting ComicCon dressed as one those guards in the white uniforms who can't shoot for shit."

"Stormtroopers," he murmured. "How do you know all this?"

"I told you. I studied you. Your grocery order, delivered at home, with way too many processed foods. The fact you watched documentaries. You didn't vote because you didn't like the candidates. Prefer crunchy peanut butter. And you tuck it to the left."

"There's no way you know that," he blustered, reeling from the fact she knew him all too well.

"It's not hard to figure out. Only had to look at a few pictures. For a scrawny puss, you were packing."

"Were?" He arched a brow and thought it interesting that she turned her gaze away from him.

"Haven't been able to tell if it's grown with the rest of you."

"In the pursuit of science, by all means, have a peek." He knew he had nothing to be ashamed of down there.

She changed the subject instead. "On another topic, I want to say congrats on not killing anyone yesterday."

"Only because you stopped me."

"P-p-please." She rolled the p. "Given your level of hostility, you were being downright gentle."

"I'm pretty sure the guard I tried to choke would disagree."

She waved a hand. "Wade? He was a bit of a douchebag, and it was perfectly understandable, given your jealousy."

"I was not jealous," he lied.

"So you wouldn't freak out at all if I said I went to see Wade afterwards and gave him a blow job in apology."

Marcus didn't realize he'd punched the concrete wall until the pain radiated from his fist. He sucked the bleeding knuckles and refused to look at her.

"Just so you know, I didn't actually do that, so no need to kill Wade next time you see him."

"Maybe I'll just kill him for being a twat," he grumbled.

"I don't think too many would blame you. But even given his epic douchebaggery, you didn't immediately snap his neck."

Because Marcus enjoyed watching the light slowly fade from his eyes. "I attacked the guards that came after."

"Again, not killing any."

"You did see me toss one into the wall, right?"

"Toss, yes. Twisted his neck? No. Nor did you tear into anyone."

The observation brought a frown. "But I could have." He'd done it before.

As if she read his mind, Jayda said, "I watched the video of your escape."

"Don't you mean Chimera's release program?" Unable to hide the disgust he'd not seen through it. He'd known it seemed too easy, the power failure that last only seconds, long enough to shove the door of his cage open.

"Adrian has ideas about treatment that don't always mesh with the doctors. Sometimes, he has to manipulate events to prove theories."

"And what did releasing a bunch of monsters prove?"

Rather than reply, she posed a question of her own. "Did you know of all the projects that escaped during that time, there's only one that hasn't come back? Maybe you've seen her. Female. Petite. Tanned skin, dark hair."

"I know who she is. She's dead." Or no longer able to walk on land. Last time he'd seen Matterra, tentacles had sprouted from all over her body and she'd jumped into a river in the mountains, never to be seen again. As to the others, Jayda was correct. One by one, they slipped away from the strange pack they'd formed during their escape. He'd assumed they'd gone their own ways.

"Odd thing that, all of you returning. Don't you think? No one can figure it out. It's why my dad had one of you autopsied."

"Only one? I find that hard to believe given how many have been killed to keep the clinic's secret."

"How many would you kill if you thought it would hand you your freedom?" she countered.

"Not the same."

"You're right. It's not. In life, we tend to treat our own lives as the least important of all. What I'm trying to do, though, is point out that sometimes you do what you have to."

"Which is why your dad has guys autopsied to figure out where the science went wrong." Said sarcastically and yet she nodded.

"He does, but if it makes your queasy mind feel better, he only had one executed. Dude went over the edge. Took out a guard by ripping into his jugular and eating him. Couldn't feed him regular carbs after that."

"So he was murdered in the name of science."

"Around here, the correct term is donated his life." Her smile was cold. "They took him apart and examined every bit. Did that to the ones they caught in the woods, too. Do you know what they discovered from all the bodies they examined?"

Despite himself, curiosity stirred. "What?"

She shrugged. "Nothing. Nothing at all. Every single one of the projects who returned had no reason to come back. Not a physical one that we could locate. And trust me, they tried. I've seen the reports. They compared everything, even the contents of their bowels."

"You said some were caught. Did you ask them?"

"Not me. My dad tried. So did Adrian and Sphinx and a few others. It didn't pan out. Thing is you're the first one that's actually been capable of real speech. So let me ask you, why did you come back?"

How to explain something he still didn't grasp. He bared his teeth in a savage smile and said, "Revenge!"

"I'm sure that played part of it. Yet, again, I've seen the footage. You watched the place for over a week. Never attacked anyone. Hid when the guards went looking in the woods."

"I was biding my time." Waiting for something. Someone...A glance at her should have resulted in a glare, but he could only admire the casual ease she displayed talking with him.

How long since he'd had such an open conversation with anyone? He'd spent most of his time since waking from the coma angry. Ranting. Not listening or wanting to listen.

Until Jayda.

"Let's backtrack a bit. After your escape, what did you do? Did you ever try and leave the forest or mountains?"

"No." He ran, and for a while, he wasn't aware of much.

"Did you find anyone?"

"Not a single soul." The one road he ran across panicked him and sent him fleeing deeper into the woods.

"How did you survive?"

By being the monster they made him into. He didn't want to explain his shame. Of how he lived literally like an animal. But again, she knew.

Understood because she claimed to be a monster, too.

"Let me guess. You hunted, hid, and rested. Until you were called to return."

Her use of the word call brought a frown. "What do you mean?"

"Did you ever hear a voice? Someone telling you to come back?"

"No."

"Are you sure?" she insisted.

"No voices. I'm not crazy." Spoken harshly. Then remorse set in, so he softly admitted, "It was an urge at first."

"An urge to do what?"

His shoulders rolled, and he couldn't look at her as he tried to recapture the feeling so he could explain it. "At first it was like a fond memory. It keeps playing over and over, lulling you into remembering the good, not the bad. It has you longing, and you think, I should go back for a visit."

"But you didn't immediately heed the call," she prodded.

A shake of his head sent golden locks flying. More hair than he'd ever had in his life and the gold not because of any chemicals. "I tried to ignore it. Because I knew it was crazy. I didn't want to come back." He looked around at the concrete walls.

"Do you think they've created some kind of signal to call the patients back?" she asked.

He frowned. "Is it possible?" Canines had the ability to hear on wavelengths humans couldn't.

"If they did, then why do they keep scratching their heads? No." She rolled to her back and stared at his ceiling. "I think it's something else."

"Masochism?" he offered. Only partly jesting. He knew what the clinic would do to him, and yet the need became all-consuming. He returned, and no surprise, look where he ended up.

"I don't think you're a guy who's into pain for shits and giggles." She turned to look at him, head propped on an arm. "But I do believe you were lonely."

"The quiet was nice. Now, I can't have an hour myself without someone interrupting and blabbing."

"Is this your way of saying you need me to leave so you can use the washroom? I did wake you up. You probably have to pee."

Heat pulled at his cheeks. "No!" Which was a lie. He had to go something fierce; however, while he might have been pissing in a cave a week ago, for some reason, talking bodily functions with Jayda was just wrong.

"So you did have an erection," she exclaimed.

His cheeks caught fire. "No."

"Then you have to pee."

He saw the trap and glared. "Go away."

"Okay. But I'll be back in like fifteen minutes. With breakfast. So, if you gotta go, go. Here. To help you out." She rolled off the bed and tossed something at the camera, which stuck.

He blinked as she waved before walking out the door.

Remembering her threat about returning, he took a minute to quickly take care of his business, especially since the glob she'd placed over the camera began to slide down. The sink had running water, lukewarm, but welcome. He splashed it on his face, rinsing himself even though he didn't appear dirty. He wore clean scrubs, different ones than before. His hair was washed and brushed, which meant they'd groomed him while he slept. Moved his room, too.

A glance at the bed showed no restraints. No weapons either. The entire room appeared almost made of a seamless mass. The walls, ceiling, and floor of poured concrete. The lights overhead high enough he couldn't reach them if he jumped. The camera was embedded into the wall, the red eye showing again since the wad of slime hit the floor. She'd come prepared.

Prepared for what?

Jayda had him all turned around. Her attitude with him so different from everyone else. For one, she spoke to him as if he were normal.

And he reacted to her as if he stood a chance. It was an attraction that would go nowhere. He shouldn't lose sight of the fact that, for all her flirting, Jayda worked for the clinic. Everything she did probably benefitted her father.

He had to resist.

Had to say... "Is that waffles?" His eyes lit up as she entered the room balancing a tray. It never even occurred to him to rush her, throw her to the ground, and leap over her in a mad dash through the door for freedom.

"With whipped cream."

And strawberries, plus a pitcher of real maple syrup.

He'd escape later. Marcus suddenly found his appetite. Snaring the tray, he set it on the solid concrete table and dug in with more appetite than he'd had...since before his accident.

"Aha. I knew it," she crowed, sitting across from him.

"Knew what?" he asked in between shoveling food and guzzling the orange juice.

"Those idiots were feeding you bran and prune juice, weren't they?" She slapped her thigh.

His lips quirked. "No. They even offered me bacon."

"Which you refused. So why you eating now, kitty?"

As if she didn't know. "Maybe I'm finally hungry again." Which was the truth. After starving for so long and losing all interest in food, suddenly things tempted again. He savored the sweetness melting on his tongue.

"Next time I'll bring extra whip cream." She lounged against the wall with a pleased smile on her lips.

"You keep assuming a next time."

"Yup. Because, let's be honest, you're not going anywhere yet. Which means you and I are gonna become friends."

"Friends don't lock each other up."

"They do if they have a safe word." She winked before shoving herself from the wall. "Now that you're done stuffing your face, I wanna go back over what you were saying before. About how you were drawn here. I don't suppose you remember any weird dreams around that time?"

"I don't dream." Not humanly anyway. He did often get the impression he was running. Running so fast, and sometimes roaring. Then he'd wake up, his heart pounding, his hair bristling all over his body. "Nor do I get visions. I don't hear a heavenly voice. My return here is nothing but a stupid lapse of judgement because, apparently, I am more masochistic than I realized."

"Nothing wrong with a bit of pain during pleasure." She winked before pivoting so that she could pace. "Where would you go if you could escape again?"

"Why bother? You said it yourself; I'll probably end up coming back."

"Not all the projects do. Luke disappeared months ago and has yet to return."

Even Marcus had heard of Luke, the very first wounded soldier to get treatment, if you didn't count Chimera himself. "I thought he was locked up and considered crazy."

"Turns out all he needed was the right nurse to snap him out of it."

"How did she treat him?" he asked, curious despite himself.

"She didn't. Not with drugs or anything, at least, unless you count her lubricating his dick with her honey."

"His nurse had sex with him! But he was her patient." The idea shocked.

"Anywhere else their relationship would have gotten shut down. But Adrian and my daddy, they believe in love."

He snorted. "More like they want to see if their cure leads to viable babies."

"That too." She didn't even deny it.

"So what's the theory with Luke? That sex fixed him?" What a fascinating concept.

"Would have to be some magical pussy."

"I think I should try." She whirled at his words, and on an impulse, he said, "Think that hot night nurse would have sex with me?"

If he'd hoped for a jealous explosion, he was disappointed. "Sorry, kitty, but she just got put onto a new rotation. But I'm sure we can find someone for you."

She didn't offer herself. Surely, he wasn't disappointed. "I'm just kidding. I don't want someone taking care of me." Mostly because he feared the beast would become too tempted. The meat sacks smelled so yummy. Jayda smelled even more delicious than them. He clenched his fists and regained control before she noticed anything untoward.

"No worries." She snorted. "Ain't no one going to wipe your ass. About time you took responsibility for yourself."

"Meaning?"

"Meaning it's time you took an interest in yourself, kitty. Help us to help you."

That drew a snort. "That's priceless. You want me to participate in my own destruction."

"Or you could see it as redemption. A second chance."

"A second chance to do what?"

She headed for the door, round ass captivating as she tossed over her shoulder, "Anything you want."

What if he wanted her?

CHAPTER FIFTEEN

Despite an urge begging her to stay, Jayda left Marcus, returning later that day only to drop off a tablet with his file. She didn't stay long, choosing instead to give him space. The silence he claimed to crave.

It didn't take him long to realize she'd given him a treasure with the tablet. He read what she gave him. Read it over and over. His own file, with all the information they'd gathered. Plus, images.

From the screen in her suite, she watched Marcus, his fascination with the pictures of himself before everything happened. Then the footage of him in bed in the regular hospital. Tubes running into his mouth and arms. A bandage wrapped around his head, his eyes closed, and his body small, shrunken, weak.

Pictures that looked nothing like the now. There were a couple for him to browse, and he did so, staring at himself, even enlarging the image at times and shaking his head.

As if he didn't believe, he sought proof. The tablet had a camera, which meant he could see himself. A man he didn't recognize, given how he touched his face, running fingers over his brow and cheek. He lifted his hair even, pulled at the golden strands, and frowned at it.

When he was done studying his file, Jayda ensured more files appeared for him to study. Successes and failures. Fascinating stuff. Especially seeing how some didn't get off as lucky, their bodies irrevocably changed as they lost the fight to stay human. The lake had more than a few that couldn't survive on land anymore. Becky, their first true aquatic success, had to spend time every few days submerged. In a sense, she and Marcus were the lucky ones. They could at least pass as human.

For now.

Would the beast within end up consuming Marcus? Too soon to tell. What she could test was his supposed return to sanity. She stayed away for three days.

Three days of not being in the same room. Not talking. Nothing. All she could do was spy. By the third day, she noticed him beginning to grow very restless, agitated. Pacing with barely controlled energy. His body thicker than previously. His expression sullen.

Out of curiosity, she sent a woman in, a pretty Filipino with limited English to clean his room. He bared his teeth at her and retreated to a corner. Not attacking. Not paying her any mind at all, despite the fact the woman bent over more than once.

But one woman wasn't a true test. She sent in a nurse next, an attractive blonde who simply asked Marcus if she could get a urine sample. He threw the plastic bottle at her and chased her from the room. Unharmed.

The guard, on the other hand, got roared at and barely missed getting his head popped off like a dandelion.

Jayda walked in as Marcus gripped Brady—the guard who'd volunteered for a thousand bucks—by the cheeks and said simply, "Let him go."

Eyes glowing green and wild, Marcus listened, dropping the guard, who ran from the room muttering, "That deserves double the payment."

She shut the door before saying, "Hello, kitty. Did you miss me?"

He stared at her, a hulking man with a glower.

"Uh-oh, someone is pouting," she taunted.

"Grawr." He'd reverted to nonsensical roaring, and she shivered as the beast in him floated even closer to the surface.

"Don't mope. It's not attractive."

He didn't reply but turned his back on her.

"Is someone miffed I left him alone for a few days?" She approached and placed a hand on his back. The muscles tensed, yet he didn't move or speak.

"Did you enjoy the peace and quiet? You said you missed the silence."

Nothing.

"Sorry about the food. No me means no yummy shit."

That got her a harrumph.

"Yeah, I can see you might not be liking a balanced diet. They definitely do not serve enough meat around here."

Another sound from him that might have been mirth.

"How did you like the reading material I sent?"

That drew his glance to the tablet before he pointed to himself. "Broken."

"Not anymore. The damage from the car accident was fixed."

Her claim drew his gaze back to her finally. "Different broken."

A little less beast in those last words. He was starting to respond, her mere presence drawing him out.

Me and me alone. A heady feeling. But why? She'd had her pheromones tested. Given blood, hair, and tissue. Used a different shampoo and soap before visiting him today. If it wasn't physical, why did he revive with her?

She stepped toward Marcus, who didn't move a muscle. Not even to look down at her as she stood in front of him.

The size of him might have intimidated another. She placed her hand on his chest then raised her gaze. "Yes, you are different, but you're not broken. I'd compare you more to a cyborg, except instead of fixing you with metal parts, the doctors used specific parts of animal genomes. And now you've got to learn how to coexist with those new parts. First you crawl, then you walk and run."

"And bite." He bared his teeth.

"If you bite without cause, then, yes, you are an animal," she snapped at his stubborn insistence. "An ill-trained dog that should have been taught better."

"I'm a cat. We don't listen well." His well-phrased rebuttal, laced with humor.

It lessened her irritation. "Even cats can learn,

though. Those Vegas fellows have been training big
kitties for years."

"Didn't one of them attack its trainer?"

"Yes. You going to attack me?" she asked, pacing
his room. Always aware of him, even when she gave
him her back.

"No." A word sighed with irritation. "But I
should. You're playing with me."

"If I were playing with you, you'd be wearing less
clothes and moaning my name." An idea that did
more to cream her than the last guy she took to bed.

"What do you call what you're doing?" he asked.

"Studying." She cocked her head. "I want to see
what makes you tick." Apart from her presence. Was
she some kind of cure to the feral ones?

It didn't seem likely, given the ones she'd helped
hunt in the past never stopped trying to bite her face
long enough to have a conversation.

"Pretty piss-poor observation, given I'm in a
room with fuck all to do."

"I gave you reading material, and I saw you
working out." Which didn't surprise, despite information in his file that indicated his only exercise
used to be walking two blocks to the subway or the
pizza joint a few streets over from his place. Something about the treatment made working out almost

an imperative. The body needed to expend excess energy.

"Yeah. Fun times. Guess what I'm doing later. And tomorrow. Although I am thinking of changing shit up by throwing in a nap."

The sarcasm brought a lilt to her lips "Is kitty whining he's bored?"

"I'm declaring it. I'm at the point I'm almost ready to ask for some treatments because even the wracking chills and vivid delusions would provide a break from the shitty monotony of my life."

He'd gone past verbose into downright dark poet. A nerd in a hunky body. It didn't help dispel her attraction to him.

"Well, given you're ready for a change of scenery, you'll be excited to hear we're going on a field trip."

"Going to take me out back and put me down like Old Yeller? Poke around my insides to see what makes me tick?" He arched a brow. "Sounds like fun." He held out his wrists, big enough she doubted she could wrap her fingers around them. All of him was thick.

Her gaze dipped, just for a second, but when she looked at his face again, he smoldered. Like literally. His eyes were a smoky green fire, his lips parted, and his expression utterly hungry.

He almost got shoved onto that bed for a different kind of study.

Maybe later.

First, she had a question to answer, and she wanted him around when she tested it.

"Usually, boys don't ask me for cuffs until at least our second date," she teased. "And let's be honest, do you really think we have a portable restraint that can hold you? Instead of saddling you with useless crap, we're going on the honor system."

His brow understandably wrinkled. "Excuse me?"

"Honor system. You know, where you promise you'll not attack or try to eat anybody."

"Why would I promise that?"

"For one, it gets you out of here." She cast a disparaging glance around. "Two"—she fixed him with a stare—"it shows you can be reasoned with."

"I still have yet to see how it really benefits me."

"Because if you can be rational, like you are now, then there is no need for a cage."

At that dangled treat, he shut down. His face literally shuttered.

"Actually, I do need to be locked up. You've seen what I'm capable of. I'm a killer."

"And? Everyone needs a hobby." She whirled

and headed for the door. Holding it open, she cast him a glance. "Coming?"

"Any guards who see me out and about will probably shoot first, ask questions later."

Her grin might have been a little feral when she said, "Anyone who lays a hand on you, or turns you into a tranquilized porcupine, will answer to me."

"What does it say about me that I kind of want to watch?"

"That you have great taste. Now come on. Let's go." She added a bit more wiggle to her walk than needed, knowing he watched. He also followed.

She didn't head for the elevators but rather the most secure part of section six. The lowermost floor of the building. Only the most trusted were allowed down here because this was where they kept most of the oopses.

The problem with experimental science was not every attempt turned out right.

There was a number who died. A lower number than you'd expect, especially given most who came were extremely ill, terribly injured, or simply unable to achieve full function of their body. The treatment healed, made them whole again, and—in some cases —better than whole.

But there were drawbacks.

Those who couldn't handle the side effects were kept on level six.

The wing she took him to wasn't as nice as his. This was the dirty secret of the clinic. The Aisle of Lost Souls they'd nicknamed it, where they kept those that had no need of amenities or extra space.

The monsters.

She didn't have to look to know Marcus bristled at her back as they approached the door to that most disturbing of wings.

"You're locking me up in *there*?" The way he said it meant he'd heard of the special prison.

"No, but we're visiting it."

Even though she half expected it, she still gasped in surprise as he rushed into her, whirling and pressing her against the wall by the door.

He snarled at her. "I'd rather you kill me than put me in there with the monsters."

"Stop being stupid and listen to me. I am not," she enunciated distinctly, "leaving you in there. Unless you keep insisting on being a moron."

"Swear."

"I swear, kitty. So long as you keep talking to me like this, you'll never be put in those cages." She wondered if he believed her. He certainly stared hard enough.

Knowing the cameras watched, she worried that,

at any moment, her father would ignore her demands and send guards flooding the place.

But there was no stomp of boots, and Marcus did nothing more than stare—hard enough to bore a hole —before turning to glance at the door.

"Let's see if your word is as good as mine." He released her and stepped away.

"My word is gold." And to keep it that way, she rarely made promises. Made it easier not to break them.

"Why are we going in *there*?" he asked as she pressed her hand against the scanner. It lit up, and the door released with an audible click.

"To see if it's only you that gets smarter when I'm around."

"What's that supposed to mean?"

"You'll see."

Stepping in, she glanced at the long hall, concrete for the most part, trimmed in metal. Signs labelling the sections overhead. The grate in the floor, stained a darker color, a reminder that those in this place didn't usually have a happy ending.

The despair hung thick in the air, but denser still, a skin-prickling awareness. Marcus stepped past her, his body stiff, his head turning side to side as he scented the air.

"Bad." The word growled from him.

She didn't know if he meant the place itself and its purpose or those it kept imprisoned. Maybe both. "This is where we keep those that can't be let loose." Because the spilled blood was messy to clean.

"You should go." He whirled suddenly. "Bad for you." He shoved at her, but she stood her ground.

"Don't worry, kitty. I can handle it. After all, I took you down." She winked and stepped past him, aiming for the second-to-last door. A perfect test subject.

Recently arrived from level five when he went nuts. Not too large of a patient, so easy to handle. She entered the code she'd memorized, and the door hissed as the seal loosened and the bolts slid free.

The occupant didn't rush to see her. He huddled in a corner, head tucked.

"Oh, Harold," she cajoled, stepping into the cell.

"What are you doing?" Marcus asked. "Get out of there."

"Testing a theory. My dad seems to think my presence makes you more cooperative. I wanted to call him a liar, but..." She cast him a glance. "I think we both know the truth."

"Maybe I don't talk to anyone else because they're boring."

"If you say so, kitty. Let's see if Harold feels the same." She stepped closer, and finally a head lifted, the cranium of it bereft of all but a tuft of hair. The skin displayed a grayish overtone. The enlarged ears possessed a pointed tip and the eyes that watched her were pure black.

It wasn't a blanket wrapped around Harold's body but arms with a membrane that hung down. Only as Harold stood could she see they were wings. Harold had changed since his last picture.

"Hello, Harold," she said. "I'm Jayda. Do you have an urge to talk?"

"This is dumb," Marcus hissed.

"Feeling a little like your old self?" she continued, noting how Harold never once blinked.

She stepped closer, and Marcus growled.

The noise didn't draw Harold's attention. The creepy man didn't cease his impressive starting.

Intent on bringing back his focus, Jayda snapped fingers in front of his face. "Yoo-hoo. Anyone home?"

She got her wish. The bat-man focused on Jayda, a dark, non-blinking stare. Then he lunged for her!

CHAPTER SIXTEEN

The disaster was evident the moment they entered that hall.

Jayda obviously had some point to make. Or perhaps a threat. *See where you'll be living next if you don't get a grip.*

Either way, they were in this place that smelled wrong. And she was determined to antagonize a bat-looking dude, which meant Marcus stepped in.

More like threw himself between the monster and Jayda. The bat thing hit him, and they tumbled to the floor, twisting and grappling, the vampire snapping its teeth while Marcus just struggled to keep those incisors from connecting.

It occurred to him he could easily kill the guy. It might even be a blessing, yet did he deserve such a punishment just for being unlucky in his reaction to the Chimera treatment?

Jayda dropped to her knees beside them and jabbed a giant needle into bat guy. It didn't take long before he went still.

And snored.

Marcus stood and glared at Jayda. "What the hell were you thinking? You knew it would attack."

"I thought it might, but I wanted to see for sure."

"That was dumb."

"Please. I knew you could handle him for a second while I grabbed the syringe."

"Whatever game you're playing, we're done." He moved out of the room, only to find himself stopped by her hand on his arm.

"It's not a game. Not to me. Don't you see? I had to know."

"Know what?"

She stepped closer. "If it was a pheromone thing that everyone reacts to, or just you." She glanced up at him.

"Meaning I'm the only idiot." He snorted the words.

"I don't think you're dumb." She stroked a hand down his cheek.

He caught it, held it pressed to his flesh, the touch the most intimate thing he'd felt in a long time.

"Is this another test?" he asked as she stepped closer, cupping his face.

She stood on tiptoe and whispered over his lips. "Yes. I want to see if my lips catch on fire, too."

What did she mean by "too"?

A query lost as her mouth touched his. Not just touched.

Kissed.

She kissed him, her lips slanting over his with slow and sensual decadence. Caressing and tugging, demanding more.

He grasped her around the waist, lifting her to ease the strain of her stretch, opening his mouth and tasting her, the wet slide of her tongue shiver worthy.

It wasn't the lights going out that first announced something awry—he had his eyes closed. But when the electricity cut out, so did the constant hum that meant the recirculating fans were working.

That shot his eyes open, and he cursed. "Power failure."

"Not a big deal. We've got glow strips lining all the floors." She pointed, and he noted the yellow dotted line with an arrow showing the way out.

"I'm not worried about getting out. I'm worried about *them*."

"You mean the other patients?" She glanced at

him then the door. "The doors are still locked in the event of a power outage."

"Are you sure about that?" He no sooner spoke than there was a clanking, as of a lock opening. Then a creak.

Followed by, "Uh-oh, kitty. I think we have company."

Which didn't worry him so much. Surely anything escaping would ignore others in this place in their quest for freedom.

He'd be wrong.

Clank. Click. The sound of doors being unlocked proved unnaturally loud. Louder still Jayda's voice. "Well, that doesn't sound good."

Someone had freed all the monsters.

Worried about Jayda, Marcus headed for the door, determined to be the wall against attack. Only he'd not even reached the threshold when a sinuous, long shape darted in and wound itself around his torso!

Yanked into the hall and dangled upside down, it took Marcus a moment to realize he was held by a snake. Of sorts. The tail definitely appeared anaconda like, wrapped around his midsection in coils, but by the dim light of the strips on the floor, he could see the serpentine body led to a man. His chest started past his navel. He had two arms still and a head, but his nose had flattened into simply nostrils. His cold eyes were slitted, their expression quite mad.

Which meant Marcus was somewhat braced when the tail slammed him into a wall. *Bang.* Ouch. Damn. He was airborne again, only to quickly hit the opposite wall.

"Hold on, kitty. I'm coming."

He wanted to tell Jayda to run away instead, only the coils squeezed tighter, expelling all breath. In the strange strip light, he could see her darting toward him, only to be waylaid as a misshapen creature, loping on all fours, attacked her, leaping with its jaw wide open.

It never connected.

With a dip to the side, Jayda hit it first with a hooked fist to the head. Then she grabbed it around the neck and yanked down, wrenching it while driving her knee up and connecting hard. The body —with all its wrong angles and odd face—hit the floor.

But that was only the start. More of the monsters attacked, the next one Yeti related. Jayda didn't run away from the fight. She took one step forward before ducking as a shaggy arm, the hair on it hanging in matted clumps, aimed to knock her out. She slid under and punched upward, causing the Yeti thing to squeal.

Flipping to her feet, she grabbed something on the wall, and then she was by Marcus's side, fist clenched around a new needle. She jabbed it into the tail of the snake, and that was enough to get him whipped back and forth a few times. He left his stomach behind and would need a whiplash neck brace. The thrashing stopped suddenly, and he was dropped to the floor.

His numb body and non-responsive hands were not fast enough to break his fall. The jarring pain to his face did much to snap him out of it. Circulation returned with streaks of pain in his body, and he made sense of the noise.

Thunk. Thunk. Squaw. Scree.

A shift of his head and he caught the action. Jayda danced in the hall, another needle in hand, facing off against a bird woman. And it wasn't just the cawing lady whose eyes glowed. Jayda's lit up too.

Another monster went down. And quiet resumed.

Marcus rose to his feet and noticed Jayda's chest heaving, her skin flushed.

He was also flushed.

And hard.

So very hard.

"You can fight." A statement that held much admiration.

"I hold my own." A nonchalant shrug.

It only served to fire his lust.

He strode toward her, hungry. Needing...

Marcus swept her into his arms and devoured her mouth. She met his hungry kiss with the hot clash of teeth and the sinuous slide of tongue. Aroused, he pushed her against the wall, grinding against her as their lips dueled. Need pulsed in his body.

Ached for release.

"Kitty." She moaned as she dry humped him.

The fabric in his way annoyed. He snarled as he tugged at it, and she cooed, "Slow down, kitty, we're about to have company."

"Kill 'em," he grumbled, frustrated by the pants blocking him.

"Can't kill them yet. We'll finish this later," she whispered.

He didn't realize her intent until the syringe sank into him and cold swept his body.

He sank to his knees, losing grip on her nubile

frame. Stared at her with incomprehension, frustration, and a bit of anger.

"Betrayed. Me."

"More like saved you. Again. Night, kitty."

CHAPTER SEVENTEEN

Jayda's father paced and ranted in Adrian's office. Whereas she sat in a chair, legs dangling over the arm, and waited.

When he finally drew a breath, she jumped in. "Don't be such a drama llama. Your precious failures are fine. I didn't kill any." Just used the needles she planted ahead of time to give them a nap. "Not only did they come through intact, Marcus is unharmed, and I don't have a scratch to show for it." Only a few bruises that she didn't mention. She wasn't a whiny bitch.

The success of her experiment didn't reduce the intensity of the glare one bit

"What were you thinking?" Snapped by her father. His moods were becoming more volatile of late. Signs he wasn't as in control, as he liked to claim.

"She was being a good researcher," Adrian offered. "Let's be honest, you were thinking of having her visit some of the patients to see if she had the same effect as she does on Marcus. I think she adequately proved she doesn't."

"By being dumb," her father huffed.

"Hey, things wouldn't have gone to shit if the power hadn't gone out. And even then, how was I to know the bat-man was faking it?" Turned out the little shit snuck out while she was occupied and had been the one to rip out the power line for that section and then let everyone loose.

"You would have known if you weren't busy sucking face with Marcus!"

And there it was. The real reason for her father's anger. "I thought we clarified the day after I lost my virginity that you have no say in what I do with my body."

"Well, I have a say in what you do to his." The very daddy-ish retort.

"Not in this you don't. Marcus is my concern now. You seem to forget, I don't take orders from you, right, boss?" She tossed Adrian into the fight with her father.

"Sleeping with him probably isn't a good idea, actually," Adrian said, stabbing her in the back.

She glared. "Don't you start, too. Marcus is fine."

"Fine when you're around," her father corrected.

"I wonder if he'd stay sane if we gave him something with her scent," Adrian mused aloud.

"Want me to toss him a used pair of panties?" she joked.

"That might be better than a shirt," Adrian remarked.

"Gross. And no. Jesus, did it ever occur to you that it's not my smell that is the reason why he acts that way with me?"

"He desires you," Adrian said, ignoring her father's growl.

"Yes. He does. He's a man who wants a woman. And as many other cocky peacocks, displays himself at his best around me."

"There's preening and primping, and then there's grunting and wordy discussions. You are grasping at straws. He needs you to function."

Her lips compressed. The idea of being needed flattered and frightened at once. She didn't want someone depending on her to exist.

"I'm sure there's a logical explanation."

"He's your mate." Adrian was the one who dared to say it, and in its wake deep silence, then protests.

"Like fuck," she snapped.

"The mate thing, it's a myth," her father argued.

Adrian, having tossed the bomb, shrugged. "Then how else would you explain it? From the moment she appeared, he's acted different. And look at you." Adrian jabbed a finger. "Doing everything you can to free him. Employing your feminine wiles."

"Don't you put this on me. You were the one who told me to do anything to snap him out of his funk," she countered.

"The Jayda we know would have told us to fuck off and left days ago."

It was hard to refute the truth in those words. "Maybe you don't know me as well as you thought. Did it ever occur to you that maybe I want to see him fight back the monster because it's proof it can be done?" She glanced at her father.

"Don't look at me. I'm fine."

"For now. But it's early stages yet, Daddy."

"I'm not crazy," her father reiterated.

"You were eating peanut butter this morning."

"And? It's a great protein."

"Out of the jar, with your fingers." She arched a brow. "A loss of civility can be the first sign."

"Or maybe I couldn't find a spoon."

"Sorry to interrupt what is obviously a father-daughter bonding moment, but if you're done, we have another problem we need to address." Adrian laced his fingers as he drew their attention. "Our surveillance footage shows someone sent a drone into the valley this afternoon."

"What?" She straightened, boots hitting the floor as she leaned forward.

"Our rooftop sniper took it down, but not before I'm sure it sent back some footage."

"Have the tech geeks figured out who it belonged to?" she asked, because that would be the first step.

Adrian rolled his shoulders. "Yes and no. The signal fed back to a resort in Banff. No idea which of the guests was spying."

"Could be innocent," her father espoused.

"Doubtful," she snorted. "We are not on the beaten path. Not to mention a drone capable of going a hundred or more miles away from its operator? You know what this means, right?" She directed her question at Adrian.

"Someone is on to us. We'll have to shift the more obvious part of our operations to another base until the scrutiny lessens," Adrian stated.

"Moving patients will draw attention. Especially the ones on level six." Her father shook his head.

"It would be a waste of resources to worry about them. There's a simpler solution," Jayda suggested.

Her father pressed his mouth into a flat line. "We haven't spent all that time studying them so that we can execute them."

"How about we call it scientific inquiry?" Jayda couldn't help but be a brat, knowing it would get that tic going in her father's cheek.

Adrian came to his rescue. "Before we start executing people and wiping computers, let's ensure we're not having a knee-jerk reaction. One drone means nothing."

"True. So why not double down on security for the next little bit. Also, make sure the tech guys are watching the web for conspiracy stories in the media." She'd handle peeking at the dark web to see if there was anyone asking questions they shouldn't.

"Given they might try to infiltrate other ways, I'll tell Lowry we're on a hiring freeze as well," Adrian added.

"Speaking of freezing," her father interjected, "I was supposed to head to Calgary this afternoon then Russia tomorrow. But given circumstances—"

"Don't even think of cancelling." Adrian slashed his hand. "I need you there to woo those investors." Because Daddy had just enough distinction and smooth talking to convince the rich to part with their wealth.

Her father left soon after, still grumbling, but Jayda remained behind.

"I can see your brain moving a mile a minute. Spit it out," Adrian demanded.

"Contrary to what Daddy thinks, Marcus isn't a threat. He could have let those projects tear me apart today. Could have hurt me or tried to escape. Instead, he came to my aid."

"And then you dropped his ass. Again." Adrian shook his head.

"He'll be pissed," she agreed. "But I'm going to wager he doesn't harm me."

"Wager with your life?" Adrian's brow lifted. "You know what your father would say."

"Daddy's not here. I am. And if I'm right, you're going to let me take him outside."

"Out of the question." He rapidly shook his head. "We just got him back. It's too soon. How about you take him to the aquarium instead?" Adrian's secret room with a view of the underwater world in the lake. "Or go for a daily jog around level six. At least then we can keep him contained."

"A prisoner," she corrected. "Which is where you've gone wrong with him this entire time. Marcus isn't crazy or homicidal. He's depressed." She held up a hand to forestall his rebuttal. "Before you say anything, I'm going to add his depression isn't a chemical imbalance. It's societal in nature."

"I'm going to have to sound like your father for a second and say you're not a psychologist, so you can't exactly give a diagnosis."

"Maybe not, but I understand him. Unlike you guys, I listened. He thinks he's got nothing to live for. That existing in a cell, bored, without even a glimpse of the sun, is the best his life can get. Can you imagine how soul crushing that is?"

"We gave him a second chance."

"But he feels like he's being punished. Hence why he acts out."

Adrian drummed his fingers on his desk. "Taking him outside is risky."

"Only if I'm wrong."

In the end, Adrian agreed, and as planned, her father departed on his trip.

The helicopter hadn't even left the ground before Jayda was on level six, opening Marcus's door and frowning because he still lay on his bed. Slack jawed and snoring.

Damned tranquilizers. She wondered how long they'd take to wear off. Pacing around him, she catalogued his injuries, his chest left bare to better treat him. The round discs with their wires mottled his skin in sharp contrast to the yellowing bruises. As if it had been days since the fight this morning instead of hours.

She leaned over and peeled back an eyelid. No response. She began ripping discs off his body, tearing away hair.

He didn't flinch.

It annoyed her that he slept.

She straddled him on the bed and seated her mound atop his groin. Found him hard.

Interesting. His underpants kept it tucked flat to his body, which meant she'd not seen it before climbing on top.

But why did he have a hard-on?

She leaned down, the palms of her hands flat on the mattress, framing his head. She stared at him and held herself barely a hairsbreadth from his lips. Her warm breath hit his skin. The core of her pressed hotly against him.

He grew harder.

"You faker," she whispered against his lips.

He said nothing, but now she knew.

He ignored her!

As if he'd win that game.

She rotated her hips, pushing herself against him, rolling and rubbing, giving herself a delightful friction against is hardness.

Ignoring his mouth, she chose to nibble his jaw.

It was a nice jaw. Irresistible really. Furry, too. She alternated nips with rubs of her cheek.

Still rocking on him, she dug her nails into his shoulder before tackling the lobe of his ear. Suck. Bite. Tug. All while her hips moved.

Her breath quickened. Not the easiest way to come, but just being near him gave her that extra edge of excitement.

"Stop it," he suddenly muttered and then caught her by surprise when he grabbed her, rolled them, somehow not falling off the bed, and lay atop her, eyes blazing.

"Stop what?" she asked with false innocence.

"You don't get to use me. Not after what you did."

Legs wrapped around his hips, encouraging his weight, she gave him a lazy smile. "Don't be mad, kitty. I did it for your own good." Because the guards would have arrived, seen him lip locked with her, and shot him.

"Yeah, because God forbid, you fuck a monster."

"Is that why you think I drugged you?" She laughed. "Oh kitty, how little you know. I would love to fuck you, but there are those in the clinic who are against it."

"Who? I'll kill them."

His vehemence pleased. "Don't worry. I don't plan to pay them any mind." She wiggled under him.

"Teasing again? Is this another test? See how blue my balls can get before I lose them?" he growled, and yet, despite his annoyance, he thrust against her, the damned fabric in the way.

"No test, kitty." She ran her fingers through his blond mane. "And no one is watching. I turned off the camera." Because she didn't want anyone to see she might be falling for the lionman.

"Not a bright idea telling me that," he growled. "I could kill you."

"You could, but that would be such a waste since I'm here to take you for a walk."

He froze above her. "So I'm to be executed."

At his worst-case scenario, she laughed. "Don't be so doom and gloom. No one is gonna kill you. This is a present because of what you did this morning."

"I didn't do anything."

She patted his cheek. "You are so cute when you lie. We both know you've got the hots for me."

"And if I do?" He thrust against her, a few times in quick succession, and her fingers dug into his shoulders as he applied just the right amount of pressure.

"Don't stop," she pled.

"I already told you, no using me." Abruptly, he rolled off her, and she was left without his weight, and a throbbing crotch.

"Do you really think I need you to please myself?" She caught his gaze, smirked, and then stuck a hand down her pants. The athletic wear stretchy enough to accommodate.

His gaze smoldered. His features turned into granite.

Sexiest thing ever to masturbate to.

She let her finger rub, her hips wiggling on the bed, her hand moving in her pants, drawing his notice.

His nostrils flared, and he heaved in deep breaths. His lips parted, and he exhaled hotly. All of him trembled.

Then snapped. In a moment, he covered her again, his mouth seeking hers for a hot kiss, the weight of him heavy between her legs. She removed her hand before it got squished, and he rammed against her, the hardness of him felt even between clothes.

She panted into his mouth and made a sound as he rolled to his side, keeping them latched together. He did it to give himself room. His hand thrust past the waistband of her pants and dug through the hair on her mound, before seeking the heated moistness between her thighs.

He stroked her. His finger rubbing back and forth across a clit already swollen and ready.

She thrust against his hand, aching for it. He thrust a finger into her and worked her with his thumb. Then two fingers. It was the third that stretched her just right. She came. Rippling with pleasure.

Crying into his mouth. Then calming.

Clutching at him. At a loss for words. She'd never been masturbated to orgasm before by a man.

Never lost so much control.

"That was amazing," she finally managed to say against his lips.

"I know." He pulled away from her and casually sauntered to the sink to wash his hand. "Now about that walk?"

CHAPTER EIGHTEEN

Playing it cool was all Marcus had. The hardest thing he'd ever done. Harder even than his cock a few minutes ago.

He still couldn't believe what had just happened. He'd pounced on Jayda and then not just kissed her but made her come on his fingers.

That had never happened before. Ever. He wasn't a suave Casanova with women. But somehow with Jayda he knew all the right moves. It shocked that she responded so passionately to him. She'd seen the monster. Seen what he was.

Yet, she kept flirting. Teased.

Asked him to act. Then orgasmed all over his hand.

Was it any wonder he came in his pants? Problem was he had no way to hide it, hence his race

to the sink, rinsing the scent of her from his fingers—
which almost made him sob—then pretending to
splash himself. The water dripping down his chest
and soaking into his thin scrubs. Hiding the evidence
of his less-than-manly action.

When he turned around, it was to almost let out
a yell because she stood right there. Close enough
to touch.

"Jesus, baby, are you always this clingy after?"
He purposely used the nickname she hated to give
himself distance.

"You're wet." She ran a finger down his chest to
the waistband of his pants.

"I'll change." He whirled from her and stripped.
Hoping she'd leave. As if. She watched him pull on
fresh track pants and a shirt. Then laughed as his
stomach grumbled.

"Better eat, kitty. You'll need that energy
for later."

Meaning what? She never did explain, just
sashayed to the door, leaving him to follow.

But he paused at the threshold. Last time they'd
left, she tried to prove a point. Why did it feel like
she did it again?

She paused and peeked at him. "Coming?"

Already have. He almost burst out laughing.
How surreal his existence seemed. He'd gone from

hating himself and hating life to...enjoying it. He'd just pleasured the most beautiful woman.

Nothing in his past could compare to that.

He joined her, conscious of the fact he wore no chains. Not a single guard followed them. He still didn't dare believe when they entered the elevator, which stopped to let on people who gazed at him curiously but didn't say a word.

They exited on a floor he'd never seen before. A section of it set up with gaming chairs and consoles that surprisingly didn't appeal. Couches in front of a big movie-type screen. Then trestle tables and benches, partially occupied with people eating off trays.

Walking by, Jayda snared a few things: an apple, a bottle of vitamin water, a chicken leg. That almost got a protest until the guy saw who stole it.

The filched goods were given to Marcus. Except for the apple. She ate it, her lips parting to bite that smooth, red flesh.

He hurried to chew on his chicken leg, the flavors bursting on his tongue. The flavored water proved a nice chaser and precluded conversation as they took the elevator up. Next thing he knew, they were outside.

And he wasn't running for his life or being shot

at. Didn't wear any kind of restraint. Felt kind of weird, truth be told.

The late afternoon sun kissed his skin, and he raised his face into its rays. Breathed deep.

"Nothing beats the real thing, eh, kitty."

"You don't realize how much you miss simple things like fresh air and daylight until it's taken away." When he was a gamer, he didn't care if he played all night and slept all day. That his one-bedroom apartment needed a deep clean.

"Now what?" he asked. "You took me outside and I didn't kill anyone. What's next? Back to the cell where I agree to be a good boy and let the doctors do a bunch more tests?" He'd agree to anything if it meant getting his hand down her pants again.

"How about a walk by the lake?"

The suggestion sounded so very odd. Yet she strode off, not once looking back at him. He could have taken off running. He was fast enough to outpace just about anyone. Except a bullet.

But according to her, this was a test. If he passed, would he really get a chance at freedom? It seemed impossible. She played him. This was a trick. *Run. Get away.*

Why the fuck was he following her, taking long strides to catch up?

"What's really going on? Why are we really outside?" he asked, because nothing made sense anymore.

"Because it's a nice day."

"Bullshit."

"Fine. You caught me. I have nefarious plans for you." She cast him a side-glance. "But first we need to find a big bush or rock to hide behind so we can indulge in round two."

He might have stumbled. "Excuse me?"

"Such manners. Good thing I remember the wild man." She cast him a sly glance. "I like him."

Like. As in liked Marcus. The beast.

"What happened in my room was dangerous," he said, woodenly. Hating that he felt a need to warn her.

"I'm sure it was. For both of us." She changed topic suddenly. "There's Jett."

"Who's Jett?" He looked ahead and saw a man dressed in black kneeling by the shore of the lake.

"Jett is Adrian's right-hand man."

"What's he doing?" Marcus asked, noticing the guy held a towel.

"Waiting for Becky, his girlfriend, to finish her swim."

Casting a glance out over the still waters, he

frowned. "I don't see anyone." Had this Becky drowned?

"Of course, you don't. She's underwater."

And apparently didn't need to breathe because a head never broke the surface.

"Is she—" He didn't know how to finish the sentence.

"She's a mermaid. More or less. Her legs don't fuse together into a tail, but she does get scales on her skin, and she can swim with the fishies. Talk to them, too, although Dad says she claims they have nothing really interesting to say."

A mermaid. "Another monster." Said with a weary sigh.

"Not according to Jett. The man thinks the world of her. Which, if you know Jett, is like a huge compliment. He doesn't like anyone."

Well, he certainly liked his mermaid. His face broke into a grin when a body suddenly vaulted from the water, right into the waiting towel.

The guy strode off with his wet prize, and that was when it hit Marcus. "She's not locked up?"

"Nope."

The very concept blew his mind. Because this was proof that it might be possible. "How many people like me, people who were changed, don't have to live as prisoners?"

"More than you'd think."

Mind blown again. "How?" How could he, too, become one of those lucky people?

"I told you, kitty. It's all about control, which you're showing a lot of. You haven't even looked cross-eyed at anyone since we left your room."

As if he would pay any mind to anyone else. Jayda's presence consumed him.

"How long before I can come and go as I please?"

She shrugged as they continued to stroll. "Depends."

"On?"

"How well you make me come again." Grabbing him by the hand, she dragged him past a boulder on the edge of the lake. Just past it a lush patch of grass awaited. She dropped to her knees and tugged him down to join her.

"I don't understand," he breathed against her mouth. Women didn't just come on to him. Not Marcus Bouvier. They were more likely to wrinkle their noses or claim there wasn't enough alcohol in the world. Was it any wonder he'd only ever been with two women in his life?

"I." Kiss. "Want." Smooch. "You." She laced her arms around his neck, the statement making him feel bigger and stronger than any rage could.

There was something ego stroking about being desired. Chased even.

She thrust him down onto the ground and pounced atop him, lips mashed and moving.

But he still had questions. "Why me?" Was it because she had a fetish for fucking a monster?

"Because I just can't seem to resist you." She tugged off her shirt, leaving her clad only in a bra. Her semi-nudity erased all other questions in his mind.

"What are you doing?" A husky demand.

"Seducing you. You going to cooperate or force me to get rough?" She arched a brow.

Resistance was futile. He dragged her into his arms, giving her lips a taste. The remnants of her apple sweet. But the musk of her, the very scent, sweeter still.

His lips slanted over hers, nibbling and sucking, and she replied in kind, just as passionately. The scent of her desire coiling around him. Marcus groaned, and she chuckled softly on his lips.

"Oh, kitty." A soft murmur before her tongue came out to play. Slipping into the warm recess of his mouth, marking him with the taste of her. The essence.

But only when he rolled her so she lay on the ground could he touch her like he craved.

And almost feared.

It seemed impossible that his hands could skim the curves he'd fantasized about. He wasn't alone in touching. Her hands roved him, learning the nuances of his shape, sliding under his shirt to brand his bare skin.

When she shoved him to the ground, he didn't protest, rather welcomed her body atop his, her thighs straddling him. She took control. A good thing since he was consumed by her.

The kiss turned ferocious, with her sharp teeth nipping. He cupped her ass, the thin fabric of her athletic pants meaning he felt the heat radiating from her.

She ground against him in a tease that brought him to a hard erection. He wanted nothing more than to strip her and fuck her.

But he held back, also finding enjoyment in simply breathing her in. Stroking the bare skin of her back.

Choking as she shoved a bra-clad breast against his mouth. "Suck me," she demanded.

And he couldn't say no.

He suckled at the fabric cup, teasing her nipple until it protruded. Tempted.

He wanted to feel that dark berry in his mouth. Without impediment. For all his agility in the woods, his hands shook as he tried to unclasp her bra, the seamless fabric frustrating him.

"It's a sports bra, kitty. You have to pull it up." Said with a husky chuckle.

With clear instructions, it proved simple to roll the fabric away from her breasts, setting her free.

This time when he fell on her, her body trembled. She gasped at his callused touch, especially the thumb that brushed over an erect tip.

He sucked the berry and bit down, growing in pleasure when she cried out.

He cupped her breasts, enjoying their soft roundness, nuzzling the nipples, sucking at them, passing back and forth.

She grabbed at him, tugged at his shirt, and he obliged, tearing it off his back, pulling her close enough the tips of her breasts rubbed against him.

It took him a second—his mind distracted because of what her tongue currently did in his mouth—to realize her hands tugged at his pants. Shoved them down over his hips, freeing him. For a second. Then she grabbed hold of him. Fisted him. Stroked him back and forth.

He couldn't help but thrust his hips into her grip, gasping into her mouth.

"You going to take my pants off?" she asked. A whisper of promise brushed his lips.

Hell yeah. He quickly stripped her, sliding her free of those stretchy pants. The panties did little to cover her and proved fragile. Grabbing hold of them resulted in them tearing free.

The scrap in his hand proved sobering. He was strong. Perhaps too strong to truly go through with this and not hurt her.

The beast couldn't have his beauty.

He went to rise, only she grabbed hold of him.

"Where are you going?"

"I shouldn't." He shook his head.

"Why not?"

"What if I hurt you?"

She uttered a chuckle. "Kitty, I'm more worried about hurting you. Do you have any idea how hard it is to hold back when you touch me?"

The words surprised him. "You want to touch me?" He sank back to his knees in front of her.

"More than you can imagine. I want you inside of me." She turned around in front of him, still on her knees, making it easy for her to bend forward. Presenting herself to him.

The core of her.

Nirvana.

He swallowed hard. "Fuck me." Spoken almost like a prayer.

She peered over her shoulder in a come-hither glance. "Don't you mean fuck me? I'm waiting."

Sassy invitation, and yet he wasn't about to say no. His cock led the way, jutting proudly from his loins. Aching to feel her.

Positioning himself behind her, he was aware of how much larger than her he was. He needed to be careful.

So very, very careful.

He placed a hand on her hip, palming the skin. She shivered. He could smell her desire. See it in the wet glisten of her cleft.

He leaned in for a lick.

She gasped.

She'd do more than that before he was done. He kept licking, flicking his tongue over her swollen button, tonguing between her nether lips.

She gasped and wiggled. Writhed with real arousal. He pleased her. Pleased her so well, she went rigid and came, exhaling a series of "Ohmygod, ohmygod, ohmyfuckinggod."

Oh, hell yeah. Rising, he couldn't help but tease his head against her, wanting to chant himself at the feel of her. The sight even was too much. His cock touching her so intimately. But did he dare go any further?

He'd held himself in check so far, but the strain

was palpable. He practically shook with need. If he let go even a little bit, he might explode.

Jayda didn't care. "Your turn." She rammed herself back onto him, sheathing him in one fell swoop. Almost jolted the orgasm right out of him

As it was, he arched, which thrust him deeper. He threw his head back and let out a sound that might have been a partial roar.

He wanted to take it easy, to let her adjust to his size. She would have none of it. She rocked. Forwards, backwards, driving herself onto him, squeezing him so tight in ecstasy.

She kept slamming, and he matched her pace, making each stroke a little harder when he thrust. And she keened. Each time he went deep, she cried out.

So he hit that spot, again and again. She lost it, crying out and panting, not even trying to hide her pleasure. When she came, it was a wet tsunami. It coated his cock in lava honey, drawing his own cry of release. He thrust deep one last time. Came.

Shuddered with the pleasure of it.

Could barely breathe. All his senses reeled, which was why it took a second to realize the explosions he was hearing wasn't from the sex.

"Someone's attacking the clinic."

CHAPTER NINETEEN

Jayda no sooner announced it than she'd righted her clothes and was walking toward the clinic.

"Um, baby, I think you're headed the wrong way."

She cast him a glare. "Don't call me baby, *kitty*." A warning spoken with a smirk. "Let's go see who's visiting."

"I say we don't. Safety is this way." He pointed deeper into the forest.

"Safety?" She snorted. "Hello, not all of us are pussies." She insulted his manhood, the quickest way to get anyone to move. They'd wandered a fair distance from the clinic, and during their tryst, twilight had fallen, the best time for taking a place by surprise.

Without looking back, and standing tall, she strode in the direction of the gunfire. Toward the screams. Someone was shot and wouldn't shut up about it.

"It's not cowardly to avoid bullets. They hurt, and in case you haven't noticed, we don't have a gun." Despite his argument, Marcus kept pace with her.

"Don't need a gun. Just gotta be wily, kitty." She winked over her shoulder.

"Wily can't outrun a speeding bullet, *baby*." Emphasized with a growl.

"Better hope you're fast, because you call me baby again and I'll rip out your tongue and feed it to the crows."

"That's aggressive."

"So's my foreplay, and I didn't hear you complaining."

"Only an idiot would have any complaint. I like it when you let go. Would like to do it again," he added. "But that seems more likely if we don't try and stop the men shooting up the clinic."

"Who says they're all men? Woman can be killers, too." Her last words before she broke into a run.

She weaved along the open field, the grass a little longer, given fall had arrived. She ran as if the wind were at her back. Her steps light and her pace rapid. Marcus had a hard time keeping up, because, yes, he damned well followed.

She knew him well enough to predict he wouldn't let her go into danger on her own.

Emerging from the tree line, she stumbled upon a shooter dressed in camouflage. Focused on the clinic, he never saw her coming.

Jayda pounced on him, literally. Grabbed hold of his head and twisted. No second chances, no hesitation. One down. A whole bunch more to go.

Off she flew, lightning quick, her adrenaline racing in her veins. Marcus trailed her, not acting so much as observing. Which was fine. For now.

He'd have to help out soon. Overhead, the hum of a helicopter added to the chaos.

But she couldn't do anything about it. The men on the ground, though. There were quite a few, some kneeling and firing, a few prone, taken out in the initial attack. They appeared as a unit, dressed in camo gear and easily distinguished from the institute guards all dressed in black.

Where they came from would have to be answered later. As would the how and why. Right now, protecting the clinic—survival—was all that mattered.

She ran toward another man, knowing she was

about to kill again. Wondering how she'd explain to Marcus that she had permission to attack. To take lives.

How to make him understand she could control her monster? He'd already seen parts of it. He just didn't seem to grasp the full extent of it. Jayda didn't often fully let herself loose. Mostly because there was a lot of screaming and crying and people making the sign of the cross when she did.

Would Marcus hate that she was part monster too? She'd told him they were alike but knew he didn't believe it because he didn't see it. She appeared so very human—on the outside.

Inside? The same wild that ran through his veins pulsed hotly through hers. An untamed side that she now let out.

Marcus would finally see it, in all its bloody violence.

Might even fear her after. Or worse, he'd hate her.

For now, he shadowed her as she hunted in the deepening darkness of the coming night. Hunched over, and breathing hard, Marcus became the silent sentinel at her back.

With another target down, she uttered a cry, that of the hunter seeking the enemy. She was answered with howls and ululations. Her allies were here. Together they would hunt. Kill.

Protect the nest.

Loping toward the building, she saw the enemy stand and aim his gun at her. She dodged left suddenly, hearing only after she moved the echo of the shot.

Silly human missed.

She wouldn't.

Her lip peeled back over her teeth, and she opened wide as she pounced.

CHAPTER TWENTY

AMIDST THE GUNFIRE, ROAR OF HELICOPTER blades, and even the shrill screams, Marcus felt remarkably calm and acute. His mind clearer than he recalled. Which meant he had no problem deciphering everything happening from the ground force that emerged from the woods in silence to attack to the air support landing on the empty helicopter pad.

It was utter chaos, and Jayda—that gorgeous idiot—ran right into it, uttering an ululating cry that raised his hackles. Especially as it turned into laughter. Crazy, maniacal laughter that was especially awful when she killed. And she killed a lot. Without hesitation or mercy. Ripping with her bare hands.

Now claws.

A monster just like me. He'd just never believed it. She seemed utterly perfect.

Still was. The fact that she appeared entertained by her killing spree was more attractive than expected.

Of course, her antics drew attention, the kind that turned the muzzle of a gun in her direction.

Oh hell no.

Marcus might have stayed out of this battle because, after all, he had no interest in helping the clinic, but no one put a bullet in his baby.

Before Marcus could think twice, or Jayda got shot, he roared. Not some puny-ass roar, but a king of the fucking jungle, reverberating all around kind of roar.

The epic sound caused more than a few to freeze. He was pretty sure someone pissed themselves.

Kind of gratifying.

He smiled—with lots of teeth—and beckoned those now staring at him.

"Come and play," said the lion to the meat sacks.

The demand only partially worked. Two guys at opposite ends of the field took aim. As for the rest?

They didn't run. They went after Jayda.

What the fuck? His surprise meant he didn't move in time and got shot, the bullet grazing his arm. He stared at the bloody furrow, then the human who'd shot it.

"Run," was the word he growled. Then he hit the ground on all fours and loped, moving faster than he could on two legs, able to twist and weave without losing his cadence.

He caught up to the man with the gun quickly, and he soon became the man with no arm.

Who knew they were so easy to tear off?

He used it to club another guy firing tranquilizers. No time for sleeping!

There were too many people fighting. To add to the confusion, he was pretty sure some of the guards were fighting each other. Traitors to the clinic.

Also allies to Marcus in a perverted sense. Enemies to Jayda, which meant they had to be dealt with.

He ran toward them, bellowing as tranquilizer darts thudded into his chest. Weak stuff. The humans underestimated what it would take to fell a lionman.

"Rawr." He let them know their grave mistake. They ran before him, fleeing his wrath, climbing into the metal birds that lifted into the night sky.

He threw his head back, his mane rippling in reply, and roared in triumph. The enemy had been sent fleeing.

"What the hell happened here?"

The words didn't distract but rather who spoke them. He turned to see Chimera himself standing amidst the carnage.

The man to blame for his state.

No bars between them. No chains holding him down.

"Hello, doctor." The guttural words spilled from his lips.

"Marcus." Said quite warily.

"I've been looking forward to us meeting again." He took a step forward.

"Do you really think that's a good idea?" Adrian asked. "My men are still around and armed."

"Can they react before I rip out your throat?" Marcus mused aloud. "What do you say we find out?" He lunged for the doctor, who proved faster than expected. Adrian dove to the side and tried words to calm the beast.

"Killing me won't help you."

"Are you sure about that?" Marcus teased. "I'm pretty hungry, and I'll bet your flesh is tasty."

"I didn't come out here to fight with you. Where's Jayda?"

The query dumped cold fear over Marcus. He whirled around and glanced at the scene of the battle. Registered the groans of the fallen. Saw the misshapen humps of those who couldn't rise again. But he didn't see or hear Jayda.

Saw only the receding lights of the chopper.

CHAPTER TWENTY-ONE

AFTER THE ATTACK, ADRIAN WENT INTO overdrive overseeing the emergency movement of the clinic. The brazen strike by parties as yet unknown meant someone was aware of them.

They know what you've done, boyo. And they're coming for you.

He ignored that nattering inner voice. He knew better than to give it power over him.

You're good at ignoring shit. How else could you live with what you've done?

Once upon a time it had been easy to tell himself he did it for the greater good. He still believed he was doing the right thing; however, he did have a few regrets. Wished he'd perhaps done things differently with some people.

But on the road to greatness, one had to expect a few bumps along the way.

While some guards cleared the grounds of bodies, feeding them to the creatures in the lake who would enjoy the change in diet, others escorted personnel to the helicopters called in at great expense to escort them to another secure location. Not home as some requested. Who knew what secrets they might divulge if allowed to go free?

Adrian was proud of what he'd accomplished. But his actions would still put him behind bars if caught.

There was a dilemma with the transport of the patients. Too many of them to move quickly. Some impossible to move at all.

What should he do?

You know what must be done.

The right answer meant killing, not in the name of science but out of fear his precious pets might be used against him. The world wasn't ready yet for the wonders he had achieved.

Incinerating the entire clinic, a failsafe already built in, would solve so many problems. Yet, for some reason, the idea left a bad taste in his mouth. He swigged some cognac to wash it away.

Instead of killing, you could instead let them loose.

Most would never make it out of these mountains. Hell, most probably wouldn't last a week. But then there were the others...

There was a brisk knock on his door. A murmur of his secretary's voice followed by a minor roar.

Not the first since the attack. Marcus had come calling rather than running away in the confusion.

Adrian sighed as he rubbed the spot between his brows. Best deal with him. Adrian hit the intercom button on his desk and said, "Let him in."

The door slid open to reveal Marcus, a big blond man with an excellent head of hair. The applications to receding hairlines and the money that might bring to fund more projects barely excited Adrian anymore. He had more pressing concerns.

Who lives? Who dies?

"I'm rather busy right now, Marcus."

Bright green eyes fixed Adrian. "Any word on Jayda?"

Adrian shook his head. "She disappeared in the fracas."

"Because they took her!" Marcus seethed. "What's the plan?"

"Evacuate. Wipe the evidence. Hide until the fracas blows over." Adrian recited the orders he'd already given numerous times at this point.

"What about Jayda? We have to rescue her," Marcus demanded.

"What's this *we* shit? You might have gotten some privileges of late, but you're still a patient here." A volatile one that could snap at any moment, like he had on the ground below when he realized Jayda was gone. After confronting Marcus, Adrian watched in disbelief as Marcus went scrounging through enemy bodies, looking for someone that might be alive enough to give him answers. And when that failed...that was when he began ripping limbs and tossing them.

Admit it, boyo, you were jealous. In a sense he was, because it kind of looked fun. A way to blow off steam, except there wasn't time to indulge himself. Adrian had to move quickly if he was going to save himself and some of the others. Instead of severing body parts, he began making calls.

Marcus slammed the desk with the flat of his hands, rocking it. "You don't want my help? Fine. But do something for Jayda. Those fuckers took her!"

"So you keep claiming. But it makes no sense. Why would they take her?" Because surely those attacking had not taken such casualties for only one woman?

Marcus pushed away from the desk and paced. "That's just it. They didn't take anyone else."

"And you know this because?" he prodded.

"Because, unlike you, I was down on the ground asking fucking questions. Once they got their hands on her, they fled."

"Why take only Jayda?" Adrian frowned. Jayda was a success story, grant you, but not one of his best. While she could behave in a civilized fashion, she didn't have a great appreciation for life. Other people's lives that was.

Taking Jayda made no sense.

Adrian's phone rang. Private number. Which wasn't unusual. He answered it, ignoring Marcus.

"Speak," he barked.

"Sir, it's Gary." The pilot for their usual helicopter. "Sorry, I didn't call sooner. I got jumped by some thugs when I landed. They took Doctor Cerberus."

Adrian's blood ran cold as the attack took on a purpose. No wonder they'd kidnapped Jayda. What better way to make the doctor bend than threaten his daughter? This wouldn't end well. For anyone. Which made his next decision easier.

He ran his hand over his desk, and the surface of it changed to a screen that said, "Please select a target."

Adrian ignored Marcus's "What are you doing?" to say, "Show me the location of Aloysius Cerberus."

A tiny pinprick of green lit and the map zoomed on the desktop, the action quelling Marcus' annoying queries.

"You had the doctor chipped." Marcus sounded so surprised. And coherent. Would it last?

"Everyone in this facility is. Although Jayda keeps managing to disable hers."

"You think she's with her father?"

"I'd say that's a fair guess given the two-prong attack. Pretty brazen, too. Which means they don't care if they draw attention."

"They don't care if they kill, either." Marcus lips tensed into a thin line.

"If they took her, then it's because they figure they need her."

"For what?"

Adrian shrugged. "I assume to control her father. Could be to study her. Or something we've not even thought of."

"I have to save her. Where is..." The light on the map blinked out.

Adrian frowned. "That's unfortunate."

"Don't say that. Tell me the signal will come back."

"I'm afraid not."

"Then I'll go to the spot they were just at. Track

them from there." Which they both knew was almost impossible.

"We've lost them." Which meant no saving the doctor. Aloysius would spill their secrets. Adrian shouldn't be around when that happened.

"No." The wild shake spun Marcus's mane in a golden halo. "I'm not giving up."

"That's your choice. But don't expect help from me." Because he needed every resource at hand.

"I can track them. I just need a ride out of here so I can start from Cerberus's last known location," Marcus stated.

For a moment Adrian thought about saying no. Hell, a bullet to Marcus's head would really be the most efficient solution.

That's it. Keep on killing because you can't handle the fact your patients talk back.

Shut up. He almost snarled it aloud. He wasn't killing anyone because, what if there was a chance Marcus could save Jayda? Or even reveal his enemy?

Adrian couldn't fight back until he knew more. But he also couldn't spare any of his loyal troops. However, he had a man standing in front of him who was motivated and expendable.

"Get on the next helicopter. The one with Lowry and crew. They're heading to the city to minimize damages." Also known as deny, deny, deny. It would take a large chunk of cash for people to forget the activity as metal birds flew in and out of the mountains. As folk appeared out of nowhere, some possibly babbling about a secret clinic and an attack.

"Thanks." Probably the first time Marcus looked grateful and not even for the second chance he'd gotten but because he could go after a woman.

A man in love—and no longer crazy.

Was that truly the simple answer to the problems they'd been having all along?

Adrian planned to explore it more once he relocated to their new location. As to the clinic that had been his home for many years now...

A pang of regret filled him as he trailed a hand over his desk one last time before grabbing his briefcase and exited to grab the last ride out of the valley.

The moment the chopper lifted, he gave the order. "Destroy it all."

CHAPTER TWENTY-TWO

Jayda woke tied to a bed. A nice one. Four posters strutted upward from the corners, the wood a varnished mahogany. The ropes around her wrists and ankles appeared to be scarves, diaphanous fabric twisted before being looped around her wrists. A small tug served to tighten the simple noose.

The lingering effects of the drugs in her system fled, and she grimaced. Shot by some of the clinic's own guards. Traitors to the cause. She'd have to track them down and kill them.

But first to figure out where she was. Who'd kidnapped her?

A part of her kind of hoped for Marcus, even as she knew the impossibility. Last she recalled she was being tossed into a helicopter, her eyelids blinking in an attempt to stave off sleep. Yet, before she lost consciousness, she remembered seeing him on the ground, fighting. Glorious and golden in the strobing lights.

Even if he had found her, he wouldn't resort to tethers. Not after what was done to him.

A turn of her head showed flames burning merrily in a stone fireplace. The bear rug in front was a nice touch. She had a bigger one in her bedroom back home.

Further scanning showed a man sitting in the chair. A big man. His skin swarthy yet much lighter than hers, his eyes a vivid blue. His expression arrogant. His beard thick and lush. As far from golden as you could get.

And human.

"She finally wakes. Not so tough after all. And here I was told you are an excellent example of your father's skill." The foreign accent proved heavy, making his words hard to follow.

She frowned. "Who the hell are you?" Because she'd never met him before.

"Petrov."

"Well, Petrov, I don't know why you thought it was a good idea to nab me, but you might want to rethink that and let me go."

Laughter boomed from him, loud and boisterous.

"After the trouble we went through acquiring you? You aren't going anywhere."

"Your optimism is cute, but misplaced. So tell me, who do you work for?"

"I am in charge," he blustered.

She eyed him. Smirked. "No, you're not. You're just a hired hand. How much did the job pay?" she asked, winding a scarf once around her wrist and watching to see what he did.

He did nothing but puff out his chest. "None of your business."

"Hope it was enough to justify the cost of all those lives. How many did you lose?"

Petrov glowered. "Shut up."

"What is it with men who can't handle the truth? You went in blind, like an idiot, thinking it would be an easy job and—"

"I was told there was only a guard on duty to watch for animals. The building itself is small."

She wanted to slap him in the forehead for being so stupid. "That building goes six stories underground. There are usually thirty guards at any given time somewhere around the complex." She took joy in pointing out his stupidity. It wasn't as if he'd live to tell anyone.

"That many guards for a research lab?" The idiot scoffed.

She almost sighed. "Didn't you do any background before swooping in?"

His stubborn expression said it all.

"It's a wonder you've lived this long," she muttered.

"Shut your mouth, woman. It's almost time."

"Time for what?" Jayda asked, winding her wrists a few more times to tighten the scarves while watching him open a laptop.

"Almost time for us to become stars."

"Excuse me?"

Petrov got up and lumbered closer. He wore a robe, his bare legs sticking out from under the hem. When he dropped the robe to the floor, he wore nothing underneath, displaying himself in all his naked hairiness.

Her lips twisted in repugnance. "Put that back on. No one wants to see your dick."

"Soon you will feel it."

She eyed it with skepticism, thick but short. So short. "Are you sure about that?"

"Silence or I'll gag you."

"You might have to, or there's a chance I'll laugh."

The man stomped toward her, his limp penis bouncing as he lost his hard-on.

She peppered him with questions. "Who hired

you? What were your exact orders?" Because once they got their hands on her, they obviously took off. Which made her wonder, had one of the treasonous guards contacted Petrov to let him know she'd exited the building? It would explain the timing.

"None of your business."

"I'm making it my business. You're obviously not law enforcement, government, or military. They would have come in demanding we lay down our arms."

Petrov snorted. "The person I work for is above such laws. And they were adamant we capture you as leverage against your father."

"My father?" She could have groaned as she realized their reason for snatching her. "You idiots think you can use me against him?"

"In a few moments, we shall do a live video feed of me beating and raping you."

Her nose wrinkled. "Isn't that kind of gross to be showing my father?"

"He needs to comply, or you will pay the consequence."

"And you're supposed to be my punisher?" She eyed him critically. "Not well liked, are you?"

"What's that supposed to mean?"

Her lips quirked. "Because a half-dozen of you maybe could have gotten the better of me, but just one man..." She gave a sharp yank, and while the fabric stretched, she grabbed hold and kept pulling until there was a crack. The post fell with a clatter to the floor.

Petrov's eyes widened. A human reaction.

She smiled. "I guess you didn't read the reports on me too well. Which reminds me, there aren't any actual reports about me because I don't leave witnesses behind." She wound the other scarf and pulled. Another post toppled, and she sat up, the scarves on her wrists fluttering.

"What are you?" he breathed, backing away. His dick turtled with fear.

"I'm the reason why someone wants my father to cooperate. Can you imagine an army of soldiers like me?" She untied her ankles as she spoke.

"You're not so tough." He found his balls and thrust out his chest. "A tiny female like you, I could kill you with a single punch."

"Go ahead and try, tough guy." She stood on the bed, testing its bounciness by rolling on the balls of her feet.

"Even if you get past me, you won't escape. My men will kill you."

"Are you sure about that? Because..." Her train of thought derailed at a distant noise.

"My men have guns," Petrov blustered.

"Can they shoot when they're scared?" she asked, stalking toward Petrov, doing her best to intimidate.

Problem being she wasn't the only predator in the house. Petrov turned his head as the noise occurred again. A sound that could mean only one thing.

"Is that a roar?" Petrov asked in confusion.

"That's my boyfriend," said with exasperation as the door was kicked open.

CHAPTER TWENTY-THREE

HER SCENT LED MARCUS UP THE STAIRS, AND knowing he was close meant nothing could get in his way. The bullet barely grazed his arm. The meat sack shook too badly to have proper aim.

The meat sack flew, despite his lack of wings, but needed to work on his landing. *Crunch.* He hit the bottom of the stairs and didn't move.

Another impediment gone. Marcus jogged up the remaining stairs and was confronted by a few sets of doors. Two open, but it was the rumble of voices behind the one that was closed that he focused on.

Stomp. Stomp. Marcus didn't bother to hide his approach. Let the meat sack he hunted know he was coming and tremble these last moments of his life.

He smashed in the door to find Jayda looking massively peeved.

"Why are you here?" she snapped, looking tousled but gorgeous, although he did wonder at the scarves tied around her wrists. Which made no sense until he saw the broken bed.

He growled, "What's going on?"

"Nothing because you interrupted." She planted her hands on her hips, eyes flashing with anger—and lust. He could feel it tugging at him. A connection to her that probably only existed in his mind and yet had led him to find her.

Marcus, despite his beastly rage, had perfect control of his tongue. "Excuse me for saving your ungrateful ass. I told you to run away from the fight."

"I don't need your help. I had this under control."

"I can see that," he stated, circling into the room, his gaze on the naked hairy man.

"Lord save me from a man with a hero complex."

The word brought a snort. "Not a hero. Not even close. Apparently finding you is my new objective."

"You idiot. You escaped the clinic. Run away. This is your chance to get away from everything."

Didn't she yet grasp *she* was his everything?

"Most women would say thank you."

She arched a brow. "I'm not most women."

"I know."

The moment was interrupted.

"You are one of the beast men her father made." Declared in a heavy accent by the meat sack—who would soon be known as dinner.

"No one made me." Doctors might have healed his body, made him stronger. But inside... "I'm Marcus." And he wasn't about to let this asshole lay one finger on Jayda. *"Mine."*

"I don't belong to you," she sassed, making the Russian-sounding thug glance away from Marcus.

Stupid move. Marcus pounced. Literally. Pinned the guy on the floor and opened his mouth wide over terrible teeth.

Made an unlionish sound when Jayda flicked his ear. "Don't eat him."

"Why not? He smells..." He dropped his nose to run a sniff over the Russian. "Like meat marinated in vodka."

"Eat him later. After he tells me where my daddy is."

"Who cares where that Frankenstein bastard is?"

Again, she flicked hard enough to hurt, and he cast her a glare. "Stop that."

"Don't talk smack about my daddy."

"Your daddy is an evil scientist."

"Still my daddy. And I want him back."

Marcus sighed and faced the Russian once more. "Tell her."

The spit that hit his cheek and slid down could have only one reply.

She didn't see it that way.

"I told you not to kill him!" she screeched.

Marcus rose and defended the only choice he had. "He spat on me." And it was gross.

"Don't be a princess. Now, because of you, I don't know how to find my daddy. Or who the person was who kidnapped him."

"I'm sure we'll find a clue. Somewhere." He looked around the bedroom, noticed the rather old décor. Lace curtains in the window and a patchwork quilt on the bed. The laptop on the dresser beckoned.

He tapped on it. The screen remained dark.

Jayda pulled drawers and dumped out the contents. More things that didn't seem to match the dead man on the floor. He surely didn't wear giant granny panties or floral muumuus.

"There's nothing here." Jayda strode for the door.

"Where are you going?"

She cast him a look over her shoulder. "To find someone who can tell me where Daddy is."

"Um. Er." He fidgeted.

She sighed. "Did you kill them all?

"I was a little pissed when I got here."

"Just one, kitty. I only needed one to question."

"We can search their bodies for clues," he offered.

"I guess," she huffed. "You coming?"

"I didn't hunt you for the last several hours to abandon you now," was his sarcastic rejoinder.

Her lips curved into a smile. "Sweet of you, kitty. But I'm a big girl. I can handle myself."

"Would it kill you to just say thanks? I was worried about you."

"I'm fine."

"Didn't seem like it when they carted your ass off in that helicopter," he grumbled.

She stopped her descent down the stairs and rose a step to bring herself even with him. "You were worried?" She sounded so surprised.

"Of course, I was worried. I thought they might have killed you." For a moment she stared at him, and he drew closer to her, wanting to taste her lips.

"Knowing the guys who attacked were dangerous, you still decided to track me down. How?" she asked, turning to skip down the remaining steps. "How did you find me?"

"I followed my nose."

"Only your nose?" she queried as they entered the hall and found another body. Dead, his pockets devoid of anything but a vape and a few crumpled dollars.

"I also kind of listened to my gut," he admitted, which played down the strangest feeling he'd ever had. Soon as the helicopter landed in the city, he'd hopped out and basically spun in all directions. Then had just known what direction she was in.

Luckily Lowry had a spare set of keys for a car they kept parked at the airfield. He hopped in and began to drive, following the tug on his senses to a farm outside the city. Would have missed it without the strange feeling he had because it was hidden from the road. Even pulling up the long drive, he'd wondered if he was in the right spot, given the house appeared dark with all the curtains and shades drawn. Yet he'd known upon seeing it that Jayda was inside.

"Just like an addict," she muttered.

"What's that supposed to mean?"

"You think you need me, so like an addict, you can always find your fix."

"That's not why I came."

"Isn't it?" She turned back to look at him. "What do you think would happen if I were to go away?"

The stutter of panic brought a frown. "I've got control over myself now."

"Do you?"

Did he? He had to wonder, given her skepticism. She gave him her back as she went into the living room, following the trail of violence he'd left behind.

"Why was that guy upstairs naked?" he asked. Jealousy still burned in him.

"Plot to torture me to force my father to cooperate." She said it so nonchalantly.

"I should kill him again," he muttered darkly, looking up at the ceiling.

"You shouldn't have killed him at all. I was just about to get him to talk."

"I can't believe the moron used scarves." He snorted.

"In Petrov's defense, no one knows about my abilities. Father made sure all knowledge of me was wiped."

"Because you're a monster, too." He still was coming to grips with it.

"I prefer the nickname the lab rats gave me: Hyena Girl. Once you hear my laughter, it's already too late." She struck a pose.

He laughed. Hard enough she scowled.

"What's so funny?"

"You pretending to be like a superhero."

"You saying I can't wear tights?"

"I'm saying you're more like a Harley Quinn. Not quite good, but not pure evil either."

The reply must have mollified because she smiled again. "Except I don't need a bat."

And he wasn't as cool as the Joker.

They searched the house, top to bottom, only to find nothing but the previous occupants stuffed in the freezer. So much for their golden years.

Returning to the bedroom, Jayda kicked the cooling body, which was beginning to stink already.

She slapped more buttons on the laptop before declaring, "There's nothing here."

"We must have missed something."

"We'll have to backtrack and figure out where these thugs are from."

"How?"

"I have my ways." Her sexy grin just about undid him. His relief in finding her had long since given way to desire.

Every time she moved he remembered her beneath him. Saw her again, undulating, crying out, making him feel—

Bing.

The bell caught their attention, and they turned to the laptop with the black screen that hadn't responded to their touch. Except it wasn't dark anymore.

A video chat window suddenly appeared, and in

it was the face of a frightened man. His eyes were wide as he yelled, "Petrov! Where are you?"

"Who is this?" Jayda moved closer and peered at the jerky motion on the screen.

"Where's Petrov? Tell him we need more soldiers. More—" The man cast a glance over his shoulder as someone screamed. A long, drawn-out sound that had the guy moaning and breathing hard. "Oh shit. Oh shit. Someone shoot him. Shoot—"

The feed went dead, and no amount of swearing or punching of the keys brought it back.

Jayda seethed as she paced. Marcus spent that time rolling Petrov in a carpet and then stuffing him in a closet. He couldn't stand to look at what he'd done. Especially knowing he'd do it again.

When Jayda finally calmed herself, he pulled the hyena's tail in saying, "You done having a hissy fit?"

That turned her glare on him. She stalked close enough to jab him in the chest. "This is your fault. If you'd just let me handle Petrov—"

"And what if you couldn't? How was I supposed to know?" Marcus snapped and yelled back.

"You shouldn't have come."

"Too fucking bad. I did because I was worried about you."

"Why?"

"Because I care."

The wrong thing to say. Her expression shut down. "You just think you do because being around me helps you."

"Bullshit. I came because I give a damn."

"Yet you didn't want to help my father."

"I don't want to bang your father," was his dry retort.

"Is that what you want?" she purred, slinking closer. "To fuck me?"

"That's not all I want."

Her brow arched. "Careful, kitty. It almost sounds like you're going to say something we'll both regret."

"I like you, Jayda." More than liked but no use freaking her out yet.

"Because you need me." Her lips turned down.

"Not in the way you think." He moved toward her, but she danced out of reach.

"I can't do this. Not now. My daddy is missing."

"Then we'll look for him together."

"You hate him," she pointed out.

"Yeah, but if it's important to you, then I'll look for him."

"No, kitty, you won't." Her expression softened, "You are going to take this chance you've been given to run."

"Run?" His brows rose with his query. "Why would I run?"

"So you can hide before they find you."

"What happened to Chimera helping me?" He sneered. "Or was that a lie?"

"He did help you. He gave you a second chance. But now it looks like it's all coming to an end. That attack today..." She shook her head. "It means someone is on to Adrian. On to all of us. Your best bet is to go into hiding."

"Are you going to hide?" Marcus asked.

"Never," the fiery answered he expected. "I'm going to hunt these fuckers down and make them regret they ever heard of my dad. But that's my vengeance. Not yours. You need to go and have a life. Without me."

The very idea hit him like a fist to the gut. No Jayda? The panic made him understand her concern though. Was his wanting to be with her truly about him being in love, or did he fear the monster's return?

"What if..." He swallowed as he admitted his trepidation. "What if I can't control myself?"

"Then we'll see each other again." Left unsaid? When she was sent to take him out.

"And if I can handle myself?"

Her lips quirked. "Then maybe if the fates align, you'll find me."

Didn't she know he'd always find her? But he didn't want to scare her. Instead he said, "You want me to go, I'll go. But give me a last kiss."

"Just a kiss?"

Actually, he'd take whatever she wanted to give. He just didn't want to leave without touching her one more time.

She let herself be pulled into his arms. Even tilted her face that he might brush a soft kiss on her lips.

As if such a simple thing could be enough. His hunger couldn't be contained. His relief at finding her poured from his lips, and she responded to his embrace. Clung to him just as tightly and whispered, "Fuck me, kitty. One last time for the road."

It didn't matter they were in a stranger's house or that there was a body in the closet. This might be the last time he'd touch Jayda, and he planned to take full advantage. The bed was right there, but he didn't care. He shoved down her pants and slid a hand between her thighs to find her slick. And wet.

He rubbed her and felt his cock hardening. He remembered all too well how it felt to be inside her. But he kept rubbing her, enjoying the slick, wet feel of her flesh. Gauging her response by the hitches of her breath and the fingers she dug into his shoulders.

She rode his hand, undulating and moaning before finally commanding him to, "Take me." She turned so that her backside faced him, and she gripped the dresser top. The roundness of her ass cheeks beckoned. He fumbled with his pants, and his cock emerged, throbbing and ready, the tip of it pearling. He pushed at the seam of her legs, her pants still caught around her thighs, making everything a little tight.

She wiggled her ass out farther, truly exposing the slickness of her sex, giving him a perfect view when it came to watching. His cock slid into her heat, her lips spreading to accommodate, the fist of her channel clutching him.

He wanted to take it slow, to savor every moment, but Jayda was impatient. Holding tight to that dresser, she rammed back against him, riding him in reverse, forcing him to grab hold and match her pace then increase it until he slammed into her. Thrust and pumped and generally went wild.

Her orgasm hit quickly, a fisting of his cock that drew a gasp and then his own pleasure as he spilled inside her. He felt so connected to her in that moment he could swear he felt her emotions, her regret.

Regret for what?

She turned and cupped his cheek with one hand, whispering, "I'm sorry, Marcus." The first time she'd ever used his name. He didn't understand until the hand he didn't see plunged a needle into his back.

When he woke, somehow lying in the bed, he didn't have to rise and search to know she was gone.

Fled without a goodbye. Not a single trace of her left behind.

Except for the wad of cash on the dresser.

The final insult.

CHAPTER TWENTY-FOUR

Leaving Marcus—after ensuring he was chipped and a surveillance team in place—seemed the right thing to do. If he reverted, then someone would see and handle it.

It just won't be me... She wasn't sure if she could deliver the killing blow. Probably the first time since her change she didn't want to.

She hoped Marcus held on to his sanity. If he did, then in a few days, maybe even a week, when she'd been gone long enough, he'd realize he was now the master in his body again. He could live his life any way he wished.

Another success story. Wouldn't Adrian be pleased. Pity it did nothing to help her own state of mind. She felt at odds now that Marcus was out of her life. Who would have thought she'd miss him? She even dreamed of him.

And in those dreams, he looked for her. Called her name.

But she kept quiet. Hugged herself tight. Didn't reply back. Just in case this wasn't a simple dream.

She kept busy searching for her father, and yet, it seemed as if he'd disappeared. She'd found the lab where he was taken. A slaughterhouse inside. The remnants of her father's suit littered the floor. But of him? Not a trace. He'd vanished. As had Adrian and his menagerie to a secret location.

Since she felt no pressing need to rejoin him, and with no clue to follow, she went home. Not the lab in the mountains that was now a smoldering ruin. It stunned her to realize Adrian had actually gone through with it and destroyed the lab—and those he couldn't move.

A drastic move, and yet she doubted he was done playing God.

If only people understood the good he was doing. She truly believed in Adrian's and her father's work. They could heal those suffering. Put an end to so much pain.

Physical pain, at least. The emotional wounds continued to plague her. The fact her father saw her as a test subject rather than a beloved daughter. The loneliness that came from being different setting her apart. The knowledge she was a killer, the evidence all around in the form of furry trophies.

Her house in South America provided some familiar comfort but didn't entirely cure her restlessness. Even forays into the jungle, where she pitted herself bare-handed against the wildlife, did nothing to help her.

Four weeks had passed since she'd last seen Marcus. Almost a month where more than a few times she wanted to call Adrian to ask if he was doing okay. Maybe even peek in on him.

To think she'd accused Marcus of being addicted. It seemed as if she was the one who couldn't leave him alone. At times she forgot herself and longed for him, her loneliness a gaping hole now bigger than before. And when those moments hit, when her monster cackled and struggled to take control, she imagined him with her. Could almost feel the warmth of him surrounding her, whispering, *Hold on, baby. I'll soon be there.*

Ugh. She was no one's baby. She didn't need Marcus. She didn't need anyone.

Although she wouldn't mind killing something to ease the stress. A thought that lulled her to sleep, only something interrupted her slumber.

She lay still in her bed, listening, straining to

figure out what had caught her attention. Her curtains billowed with a night breeze. The window opened onto the jungle, the screen keeping her safe from tiny biting insects.

But no match for an intruder.

The scent of him hit her. Unmistakable and rousing a happiness inside that had her gasping, "Kitty?"

"In the flesh, baby." He sauntered out of the shadows, just enough she could see the shape of him.

As big as ever. But his appearance was surprising. "What are you doing here?"

"I'd say that's obvious. I came to see you." He leaned against a dresser, his expression sane, his words perfectly lucid.

"Why?" Why had he returned? Why was she so happy he'd come?

"I missed you."

She closed her eyes against the softness of his claim. "What happened to you starting over?" A grumbled complaint to fight his allure.

"You wanted me to live on my own. To prove I could control my monster. It's been four weeks. And as you'll notice, I didn't revert."

"Congratulations." She was pleased he'd managed to stay sane while, at the same time, sad he no longer needed her.

"Oh, I still need you."

It was as if he'd read her mind.

She frowned. "If you can control it, then you can live your life. Free. Like you wanted."

"I plan to. With you."

"Me?" *Thump. Thump.* Her heart raced at his words, but what he asked was impossible. "If you're looking for sex, that's over. I've moved on." She lied, and his eyes widened the slightest bit.

He killed her with a smile. "No, you haven't." He strode toward her, his leonine grace more evident than ever. He stopped in front of her. "I missed you."

How she'd missed him, too. But she kept those words and emotions shoved down deep.

"I know you missed me." He reached out and brushed a strand of hair from her face, reminding her she was in bed wearing only a tank top and panties.

"I don't do relationships."

"Because the guys you usually meet can't accept you for who you are. I see you, Jayda." He cupped her cheek. "I love you."

"No." She shook her head even as her heart burst. "You can't."

"I do, and you care for me, too."

"Do not!" A hot retort and such a fucking lie. She cared all too much for this man.

He laughed. "Oh baby, I already know. I feel it.

Here." He thumped his chest. "We're connected you and I."

He said aloud what she'd dreaded and, at the same time, welcomed.

"It's what helped me find you. Remember ages ago when you asked why I went back to the clinic? I figured it out finally. You were the reason."

"I wasn't even there yet when you started haunting the place," she argued.

"Yeah, but a part of me knew you were coming. It pulled me. That need drove me and controlled me. Led me to find you. Then and now." He cupped her chin and tilted her face. "We belong together."

She wanted to fight it longer. To deny it.

Couldn't.

Because he was right. She felt the same strange pull. Wanted the same thing.

Wanted him.

She yanked him down atop her, lacing her arm around his neck and latching onto his mouth with a fierce hunger.

That he matched. With Marcus, there was no need to hold back to hide what and who she was.

They kissed, the passion between them exploding. There was no time to truly strip. Her panties were ripped in her impatience and flung to the side.

He chuckled as he unbuckled his pants. "Pity you did that. They were cute."

She crooked a finger. "They were in the way." She spread her thighs on the bed, her eyelids growing heavy with arousal as he stared at her. Erection in hand. Desire straining his body.

He covered her, the weight and heat of him welcome. The hardness of his shaft as he sank balls deep even better. The orgasm fast and sharp, with a slow descent after cradled in his arms.

A moment of peace like she'd not experienced in almost a month.

She sighed.

"That sounded pretty heavy."

"You're heavy," she grumbled, only to wrap her arms around him when he tied to shift away. "And annoying."

"Love you, too, baby."

"Oh, shut up and kiss me."

"With pleasure."

EPILOGUE

Months passed, winter covering the remains of the old clinic. Not that Jayda and Marcus returned. When they weren't flying around the world acting on tips about the whereabouts of her father, they were in South America becoming an inseparable team, both in out and of the bedroom. The tie binding them was more than just physical lust. With practice, they could talk to each other through their link. Find each other even if one got intentionally lost.

It meant they could charge higher prices on jobs where she was the brawn and he was the brain—with brawn when needed.

It was a perfect new life.

Which was why, when Valentine's Day hit, he

went all out. Flowers, chocolate, catered dinner—since neither of them could cook.

He told her to dress up, and she did, emerging from their bedroom wearing...

"Omg you're—"

"Princess Leia." She cocked a hip and posed, the slim white gown hugging her lush curves with her hair bound in buns on either side of her head.

"I love you," he gasped, hitting the floor on his knees.

She smirked as she hiked the skirt and said, "I know."

And it was only later as they lay sprawled in a heat of naked sweaty limbs that she whispered, "Love you, kitty."

THE REPORT ON MARCUS AND JAYDA INDICATED no pregnancy yet. What a shame. But Adrian had hope. Lots of it, especially after seeing the success. Marcus had come back from the edge.

Maybe there's a chance for me, too.

A slimmer one, given the woman he loved was in a coma, a sleeping beauty who just wouldn't wake up no matter how many treatments were applied.

He'd done his best to fix Jane. Failed despite his best efforts. Her lashes had yet to flutter. She still required a tube to breathe, which meant keeping her hidden was almost impossible.

He'd gone into hiding after his lab was destroyed, and Adrian wondered if it were better to kill her now before he completely lost all sense of control. Before his enemies closed in.

Adrian rested his hand on Jane's, her skin warm and soft to the touch. "I'm sorry, Jane. I wish I could have saved you." It was time to let her go. To let go of a foolish dream before he created any more nightmares.

He turned off the machine pumping air into her lungs then proceeded to pull the tube loose. To his surprise, her chest continued to rise and fall. Probably a delayed reaction.

He sat and held her hand as her heartbeat slowed.

Stuttered.

Stopped.

And with her death, his hope died, too.

STAY TUNED FOR *A CHIMERA'S REVENGE*.

For more books by Eve Langlais or to receive her newsletter, please visit EveLanglais.com

CPSIA information can be obtained
at www.ICGtesting.com
Printed in the USA
LVHW041806170719
624400LV00005B/598/P

9 781773 840710